"I am a virgin."

"A shame," he said.

His words were casual, but his tone wasn't. He sounded harsh. Hoarse. As if speaking them had been a struggle.

And suddenly, Ariadne felt like she was being weighed down by the burden of her virginity. She had kept it all these years and for what?

She had turned off that part of herself for what?

She had stolen it from herself for nothing.

Theseus had stood between herself and Dionysus all these years. And now he was gone.

It was an entanglement she didn't need.

It was one she didn't want.

It was one she should turn away from.

"Dionysus," she said. "Kiss me."

The Diamond Club

Billion-dollar secrets behind every door...

Welcome to The Diamond Club: the world's most exclusive society, open only to the ten richest men and women alive. The suites are opulent. The service is flawless. And privacy is paramount! You'll never see the details of these billionaires' blistering romances in any of the papers—but you can read all about them right here!

Baby Worth Billions by Lynne Graham

Pregnant Princess Bride by Caitlin Crews

Greek's Forbidden Temptation by Millie Adams

Italian's Stolen Wife by Lorraine Hall

Heir Ultimatum by Michelle Smart

His Runaway Royal by Clare Connelly

Reclaimed with a Ring by Louise Fuller

Stranded and Seduced by Emmy Grayson

All available now!

GREEK'S FORBIDDEN TEMPTATION

MILLIE ADAMS

Harlequin

PRESENTS

Harlequin®
PRESENTS™

ISBN-13: 978-1-335-93900-5

Greek's Forbidden Temptation

Copyright © 2024 by Millie Adams

Recycling programs for this product may not exist in your area.

Harlequin Enterprises ULC
22 Adelaide St. West, 41st Floor
Toronto, Ontario M5H 4E3, Canada
www.Harlequin.com

Printed in Lithuania

MIX
Paper | Supporting responsible forestry
FSC® C021394

Millie Adams has always loved books. She considers herself a mix of Anne Shirley (loquacious but charming and willing to break a slate over a boy's head if need be) and Charlotte Doyle (a lady at heart but with the spirit to become a mutineer should the occasion arise). Millie lives in a small house on the edge of the woods, which she finds allows her to escape in the way she loves best—in the pages of a book. She loves intense alpha heroes and the women who dare to go toe-to-toe with them (or break a slate over their heads).

Books by Millie Adams

Harlequin Presents

His Secretly Pregnant Cinderella
The Billionaire's Baby Negotiation
A Vow to Set the Virgin Free
The Forbidden Bride He Stole

The Kings of California

The Scandal Behind the Italian's Wedding
Stealing the Promised Princess
Crowning His Innocent Assistant
The Only King to Claim Her

From Destitute to Diamonds

The Billionaire's Accidental Legacy
The Christmas the Greek Claimed Her

Visit the Author Profile page
at Harlequin.com for more titles.

CHAPTER ONE

THE EMPTY BARSTOOL next to Dionysus Katrakis was luxurious as it was tragic. It ought to be. Tragic because it was empty as the man who had once occupied it was no longer living. Luxurious because the Diamond Club was the most exclusive club on earth. With membership consisting only of nine of the world's richest men.

And one woman.

The empty chair was now for her.

And yet it wasn't.

It seemed somewhat baffling to her that there was a whole bar in this establishment that catered only to the uber elite.

You're one of them now.

But she never really would be. She wasn't the one who should be sitting here right now. And she didn't know when or if that truth would ever come forward. If there was any point to it. All she knew was that her life had changed forever. That her joy was shattered and the future they'd imagined was…

It was impossible now.

She blinked back rising tears—she really didn't want to cry right now.

And so Ariadne Katrakis took a seat on the luxury barstool next to her brother-in-law, and did not cry.

She looked at Dionysus's profile. Proud. Arrogant. Familiar. His features were arranged in the exact same order and shape her husband's had been. Stunningly handsome with a strong, square jaw, a nose that was sharp and angular. His skin was the same tawny gold, his brows heavy. His black hair was longer than his twin's, rakish, looking as if a woman had just finished running her fingers through it. Whether by design or simply because that's what had just happened, she couldn't say.

One never could with Dionysus.

Her brother-in-law was so different than her husband. Hedonistic, selfish. Unpredictable.

Horrendously likable and magnetic in spite of it all.

That was her true tragedy. She'd always felt bathed in warmth when she was in the company of Dionysus.

She imagined every woman did.

She cleared her throat.

"It's done," she said.

He turned to look at her, one dark brow raised. Yes, he was identical to Theseus. And yet he wasn't. Theseus had carried the weight of the world on his shoulders. His face had been a study in granite severity while Dionysus's was mobile. His face could cover a broad spectrum of emotion in a moment. It had always fascinated her.

"So then you've bathed in the blood of virgins and completed the requisite ritual sacrifices." The corner of his mouth curved into a smile, but she could see the exhaustion there. The grief.

"All I got was the blood of a very tired pigeon and a ritually sacrificed guinea pig, have I been misogynied?"

"I believe that is what they call *pink tax*." He picked his glass up from the bar and knocked back the remaining Scotch. "Drink? They have to get you whatever you want now. You're a member."

"Yes," she said, staring down at the marble bar-top. "I am a member."

"I apologize for everything my father said to you after the funeral."

That farce of a funeral that hadn't said a single real or deep thing about Theseus. That farce of a funeral hadn't included the people who had really mattered to him.

"Did you *hear* any of the things your father said to me?"

He tapped his glass and the bartender materialized and poured him another measure of Macallan without being asked.

The man paused and looked at her expectantly. "Just some sparkling water, please," she said.

"I didn't need to hear them," Dionysus said as her sparkling water filled the glass. "I can guess exactly what he said. I imagine he'll be fighting you for the money."

"He was thinking *you* should fight me for it."

He lifted a brow. "Because I'm so impoverished?"

"I am *slightly* richer than you now," she said.

"Amazing what hundreds of years of hoarding wealth will do." He took a drink of Scotch. "But this situation is of my father's own making, he's the one who chose to give Theseus the empire upon his marriage to you."

"Conditionally, Dionysus, which I think you know. It wasn't to be final until he produced an heir. But you did not hear…" She curled her hands into fists. "I'm pregnant."

"Pregnant?"

She didn't know if she was imagining the shock in his voice. If she was hallucinating any sort of reaction. But that was the truth. She was pregnant with Theseus's child. And that should be good news. For *everybody*. A part of him would live on.

As far as the details of all of it… She wasn't going to share them. Not with anyone.

If the truth came out the Katrakis patriarch could still disinherit her child. And that was something Theseus had wanted to avoid at all costs. He'd shaped his whole life around the desire to see the two of them at the helm of the company and to see the legacy pass on to their children, who they would raise differently than he'd been raised.

She'd made him a promise. With her whole heart, her whole life.

She would not do anything to compromise it now.

Her eyes started to fill with tears and she blinked those tears back.

He'd given her a good life. One filled with love and laughter, even if it had been unconventional. Even if there had been times she'd struggled—who didn't struggle on occasion? Who didn't regret their choices on the odd rainy Sunday?—but mostly her life had been full.

It felt desolate now, but she could not afford to be destroyed. Not now. She had the baby to think about.

"And I assume that you told my father this?"

"Of course I did. I am carrying his precious heir. You know how he favored Theseus."

There was no point sugarcoating any of it. She didn't say it to hurt Dionysus. Though honestly, she didn't think Dionysus had feelings to hurt. Not any longer.

Her current relationship with her brother-in-law was... Uneasy at best these days.

But the bedrock of their relationship was a near lifetime of friendship. They had known one another since she was ten and the boys were twelve. They had been thick as thieves growing up, anytime their families had been on the island for the summer.

She had been drawn to Theseus's quiet, serious nature, his sly wit that had flown under the radar of anyone who didn't get close enough to really listen to him. He made her laugh. He'd made her feel understood in a way no one else ever had. He listened. Really. Deeply.

Dionysus on the other hand, had been an explosion. All she could do was watch and hope that none of them got hurt by the aftermath. There had been a cheerful sort of naughty joy that he took in his exploits and she couldn't help but let herself feel a bit of delight in it too, even if from afar.

It was only after the implosion at her eighteenth birthday party that she understood his behavior wasn't just reckless…it was dangerous.

Ten years later and that was all behind them, their shared history growing up together more important than a few moments in time.

They were bonded by deeper things.

She'd been alone before Theseus and Dionysus.

And without each other, the boys had been vulnerable to the rages of their father.

Patrocles Katrakis had a mentality as ancient as the stone walls of his home country and a cruel streak as deep as the Aegean. He had exacting expectations of what he wanted from his sons. But most especially Theseus. Who was born three minutes before Dionysus, making him the focus of their father's wrath and unreasonable nature. He was shaping the son who would take over the industry.

Because that was what mattered to him most. The legacy he had built, the billion-dollar shipping company that bore the family name.

His sons were the richest twins in the world. Evidence of his virility, of his might.

A legacy nearly as ancient as Greece itself.

So he thundered, loud and often.

As Theseus's wife, Ariadne had been under her fair share of pressure. Theseus's strengths weren't in organization or admin. Or in finance, which was what James had begun to manage—and just as well because it wasn't Ariadne's strength either. Theseus was good with people. Compassionate. Things his father didn't value. But they had done a good job holding each other up as they managed the company, and their strengths complemented one another's. Patrocles, of course, minimized Ariadne's role in the company but as she'd often told Theseus, she wasn't hungry for the recognition of an old, cruel fossil.

Thank God for James. He'd been managing everything at Katrakis Shipping for the past few weeks, which seemed unfair in many ways, but he'd told her it gave him a way to matter privately.

Since he wasn't able to publicly.

And she'd desperately needed his help.

"Yes, I am aware that my father favored my brother." He laughed, a hollow sound. "Of course being favored by my father was always a poisoned chalice. As I think you know."

"Yes. I know." She looked down into her glass. "Your father approved of me as a wife for Theseus."

Dionysus laughed, the mirth in his eyes sharp, uneasy. "I am aware of that. Even still he was terribly hard on you all this time, wasn't he?"

She blinked, and looked away from Dionysus. She

was afraid they were having a shared memory. One she didn't want to have at all right now, much less share.

She needed to keep her stress managed. She'd been feeling off the last few days. Well, *off* was an understatement. She'd felt bereft since Theseus's accident. Numb. Then angry. How could the world be so cruel? They'd been ready to have their child and once they had that child...

Everything would have changed for Theseus, finally.

But her emotional exhaustion had turned into physical aches and pains that had her feeling wary.

"He doesn't want me to be in control of the company, that's for certain. He also doesn't want me being the steward of all the wealth. Sadly for him... There's nothing that he can do."

"You never struck me as someone who cared overmuch about money, Ariadne."

She wasn't. Of course, she didn't know life without it. She couldn't say how she would function, but she knew how to work. That was the thing. There were a few components to this that mattered. The first was that Theseus's legacy carry on. In the form of their child. The second was that she was able to take some of this money and put it toward causes she knew Theseus would have wanted to support.

Because there were children out there, like Theseus, who lived their lives in shadows. Who could not be themselves. Who had to hide who they were from their parents, from the world. She would…do something for them. A tribute. A charity.

She couldn't give Theseus the happy ending she'd wanted him to have, but perhaps she could take his memory and use it to make the world happier. What was the point of money if she couldn't make changes with it?

"Did he know you were pregnant?" Dionysus asked.

He'd been so happy. They all had been.

It had also started a ticking clock on the way their life was structured. She'd been excited, but nervous. Happy. Relieved.

"Yes," she said. "We found out two days before he died."

"How lucky for you that you managed to fall pregnant just before his death."

She flinched. She knew that what he said was true—if there was no baby the company wouldn't be in her care. If there was no baby none of the Katrakis money would come to her at all. But that wouldn't have been the tragedy. The tragedy was losing Theseus. The end.

"You know me better than that, and you should know I loved your brother better than that too."

His expression was contrite, which was unusual for him.

"I'm sorry," he said. "That was out of order. You didn't deserve that. The money is yours, Ariadne. My father has no right to take it from you."

"I'll be a steward of it, it will be our child's."

"You will continue to run the company. You will

maintain your position at the club. Until my nephew or niece comes of age."

His voice took on a hard edge there. It was difficult to imagine Dionysus as a doting uncle. It was difficult to imagine him doing much of anything other than making flippant remarks and indulging in excess.

What had amused her when they were younger had turned into something dangerous and frightening when they had become adults.

Dionysus had always seemed insatiable. But as Theseus went further and further into himself, Dionysus seemed to explode beneath the strictures of his father. He had gone off on his own. Had made a fortune independent of the family name.

Theseus had said he envied his brother sometimes.

Wouldn't it be nice to be my brother, flaunting conquests everywhere like prizes?

Dionysus was a libertine. She wouldn't be surprised if he couldn't count the number of women that he had taken into his bed. He might even lose track of a weekend. A forty-eight-hour orgy seemed right up his alley.

Maybe she was bitter. Bitter because Theseus worked so hard to do the right things, to stay in his father's will, to be the oldest son that fit the image.

Bitter because Dionysus seemed to have no idea. His life might be a middle finger at his father, but whether he meant it or not, also at his brother.

He was the second born.

And he was free.

Of course, Theseus could have defied his father much sooner than he'd planned. But he had spent a lifetime being conditioned to fall in line and after he'd decided that things had to change, he'd still wanted to wait until they'd had a child until the inheritance was secured, before making any drastic public moves.

"Well, given the blood rites, I *do* want to maintain my position at the club."

He chuckled. "Of course. Why would you give up all this?" He lifted up his glass and waved it around, indicating the luxurious nature of the space.

"You may not understand this, but the company actually became very meaningful to me. I know the people there. I care about them. I understand the important part our work plays in keeping the world turning. People depend on us. For their livelihoods. For survival. Under Theseus, there was quite a lot of charity work structured into the business. Employee salaries were raised, benefits packages improved. I want to keep building on what he did, and I'm the one who knows. I know it inside and out. We were a team."

"It's shocking," he said. "The suddenness of it."

"He was just going back to the office to get some paperwork. A drunk driver hit him. He wasn't speeding. He wasn't…he was himself to the end. Taking care of his responsibilities."

"A terrible waste," said Dionysus. "If one of us was going to die young, I had always thought that it would be me."

"You certainly earned it," she said.

He smiled ruefully at her. She wondered if she had gone too far, if she had crossed the line, but he didn't seem angry at all.

In fact, he seemed amused. But it was hard to say with Dionysus. She'd known him once. Really known him. They'd been friends. They'd been in-laws for a decade and she saw him casually. For dinners, holidays. They bantered, they were good at it.

There had been whole Christmas dinners where she'd lost herself sparring with him. Like the whole room had faded away and everyone else with it. But that had always been about current events or completely inconsequential topics.

They didn't *know* each other. Not anymore.

Now she felt the ache of that.

Because here they were. Without Theseus.

"It's true," he said.

"And yet, you also built your own massive business. If you didn't care about anything the way that you pretend, including your own life, why would you have done that?"

"You underestimate just how badly I wanted to prove my father wrong. About me and about everything. I made something out of nothing. My father just managed to continue to multiply a fortune that was on that path generations before he was born. I am not belittling what Theseus did with the company, or what you have done with it. But my father takes a disproportionate amount of pride in the little work that he has done."

It made sense. In a sick sort of way.

She took a sip of her sparkling water. "He would also take a disproportionate amount of pride in wresting the company back from me if we didn't technically fulfill the terms of the rather complex inheritance stipulations."

"Yes."

"He would want to automate. Get rid of as many employees as possible."

"A business is not a charity," Dionysus pointed out.

"Do you run yours with the same sort of ruthless precision your father would?"

He laughed. "That would require me to care about being rich or simply for the sake of it. And I don't. I have what I want. A portfolio of successful businesses running the gamut on practical delivery services. From car services to food and grocery delivery. It has been lucrative, and I no longer have to go in to work every day. I help people with their everyday lives, I'm able to take advantage of the fact that people will pay money for convenience, and in turn, my life is more convenient. I can do as I please."

For some reason, something about that hit Ariadne strangely. He could do as he pleased. She had so much money now. She had devoted so much of her life to her friendship with Theseus. And in all of that, she hadn't been truly satisfied with it.

She'd hoped to be.

But no one could see the future.

Maybe it wasn't Theseus who had envied Dionysus. Maybe she did.

She felt a sharp cramp low in her midsection, and she pressed her hand to her stomach.

"What's wrong?" he asked, grabbing her arm and looking at her fiercely.

"Nothing," she said.

She had been having these strange phantom pains for a couple of days, but her doctor had said they were nothing to worry about. Because they hadn't progressed, and there had been no bleeding.

"I'm just going to…" She slipped off the luxurious stool and stood up, and felt a rush of warm liquid escape her body. But it didn't stop. She was dizzy, and suddenly the pain was quite intense.

No.

This was what she'd been afraid of, more than anything, when she'd begun to ache a few days ago. When she'd been dealing with the shock of losing Theseus.

That the baby would be taken from her too.

No.

No.

The last thing she saw was Dionysus reaching out to take her in his strong arms as she lost consciousness and everything went dark.

CHAPTER TWO

DIONYSUS CURSED EVERY deity he didn't believe in as he held Ariadne in his arms for the first time in ten years.

This was not how that fantasy played out in his mind.

This was not a fantasy at all. She was dangerously pale, and now completely unconscious.

He signaled to the bartender. "Tell Lazlo I need a helicopter immediately. And have them call ahead to the hospital."

He would not be taking her to the kind of medical facility available to everyone.

Lazlo would know that. As manager of the Diamond Club and right-hand man to its founder Raj Belanger, the richest man in the world, Lazlo trafficked only in the elite, the discreet, and the luxurious.

There was no time to waste.

He knew that by the time he reached the top of the building the helicopter would be waiting. Picking Ariadne up, and holding her close to his chest, he rushed into the gilded elevator, the doors closing behind them. He felt something on his hand and looked, seeing streaks of red on his palm.

She was bleeding.

She was far too pale.

Ariadne...

Dionysus, for all the world to see, cared for nothing and no one.

The truth of him was much more complicated. He moved quickly in order to silence his demons, and he had a ready smile in order to keep a tight leash on his rage. Right now, his rage knew no bounds.

Because Theseus should be here. The world was cruel, but it had no right to be cruel to his brother, who had done the right things. Who had lived a life his father was proud of and married the perfect wife, who was supposed to have his perfect child.

Rage because Ariadne was now pale and limp and he couldn't even begin to think through what was happening to her, because if she didn't survive this...

There really would be nothing and no one in this whole world that he cared about.

Dionysus had thought, back when he had been younger, and he had longed for things to be different, that he would give any amount of fortune if Ariadne would look at him the way that she did Theseus.

But like most everyone, she had known that Theseus was the better bet for a life of stability.

And then this.

Theseus was meant to make her happy. It had been the one consolation he'd felt and even if he had no longer been as close to his brother...

He saw his brother. He had meals with him. They dined at the club often enough but they had never been truly close since the night of the engagement party.

How could they be?

Now Theseus was dead and there was no hope of repairing it. He might have despised himself then if he hadn't been so consumed with worry about Ariadne.

The elevator seemed to be taking far too long.

It arrived at the top floor, finally, and the doors opened. And the helicopter was there. He rushed across the space, holding her tightly, and climbed inside. The wind and the sound made her stir, but only just slightly.

"Hurry," he said when they got in.

And they were off. Careening over the city of London, the lights below twinkling. On their way to the only hospital he would trust with her.

If she lost the baby…

Of course, she was losing the baby. And that would mean his father would try to wrest control of the company back.

But all he cared about right now was that Ariadne lived.

He didn't care about much. He had long ago let go of the concept of anything sacred or divine. He had sold his soul for parts as he had worked tirelessly to prove his father wrong, and drink himself into oblivion just as tirelessly. Moved from one woman's bed to the next.

Yes. He had decided to fashion himself entirely after his namesake. The god of wine and debauchery.

Because why not?

He wasn't the oldest son.

But now his brother was gone.

They were only minutes away from the medical facility in Bath, formerly one of the buildings that had housed Roman Baths people used to flock to for healing. He didn't care how picturesque it was, only that they might find healing there.

Part of the building had been modernized, with a helipad on top, and when they landed a team came out quickly, and he deposited Ariadne onto a gurney, his arm suddenly feeling bereft. Empty. He looked down and saw blood staining his clothes.

He followed quickly.

Nobody tried to tell him not to follow. It would have been a foolish thing to do.

She was wheeled into a room that looked like a standard hospital room. But he supposed this was where they had to work to make her stable. And work they did.

She was hooked up to IVs, and monitors. Whole teams worked to revive her. "She hasn't lost enough blood to need a transfusion," one of the doctors said.

"Good," he said.

"She miscarried," said another doctor.

He wanted to growl and turn something over. Because it was obvious she had lost the baby. Was she going to lose her life?

She had lost this last piece of Theseus, and he felt

that pain deep inside himself. But she'd also lost this last piece of the future she'd been hoping for.

And the last piece needed for her to secure the inheritance.

Ariadne was losing everything.

"This doesn't leave the room," he said. "None of this."

"Of course," said the doctor, looking vaguely offended that Dionysus had bothered to mention the standard nondisclosure protocol of the facility.

Patient privacy was of course protected in most cases, but there was an extralegal layer of protection here, and that was essential.

It took about fifteen minutes for her to stir. It felt like hours to him.

She looked at him, oxygen tubes covering most of her expression. "What happened?"

"I'm sorry, Ariadne. You lost the baby."

He didn't see the point in hiding it from her. Even though he wanted to. Even though he wanted to cushion her from the truth. He could not allow her to lay there in hope knowing already that hope was lost.

He wouldn't do that. In honor of the friendship they'd once had. In honor of how much his brother loved her, he wouldn't do that.

And maybe even more, in honor of how much she had loved his brother.

Tears began to track down her face. "*No*," she said.

Her pain was wordless, soundless. Yet it radiated

from her. He felt it move deep inside of him and he didn't know how to shield himself from it.

She was his weakness.

She always had been.

He hadn't comforted another person in more years than he could count. He didn't have practice with connections. But she was one of the few he had.

"I'm sorry."

"This can't… There's no more… I can't have another baby."

Her eyes were red, her face streaked with tears. She was still beautiful. Another man would marry her. Another man would love her. She might not be able to imagine it now, but he knew it was true.

"You will someday."

"What about *now*?" She swallowed hard. "It was supposed to be our baby. It was supposed to be his. What about Theseus's legacy? This was his last chance. It was… It isn't just that he's lost a piece of himself wandering around in the world, he has lost all of the work that he has put into Katrakis Shipping. Everything that mattered to him. Because it did matter. This baby mattered."

"I'm sorry, Ariadne," he said.

"It was supposed to be…" She swallowed hard. "We were so happy to finally have a baby. When he died I thought the only bright spot was this baby. This… piece of him that would still live. That would walk in the world."

"If you think about it," he said, aware that he was defaulting to that shallow place inside of him that handled everything with flippancy, which had never been less appropriate than it was now, "I am a piece of him wandering in the world. We are identical. If we had planned things better, I could've assumed his identity."

The words hung heavy between them.

"You're not identical," she said.

Something about the way she said it, the disdain in her voice, made something dark twist in his chest.

"We were identical enough," he said.

Just then, the doctor came into the room. "Mrs. Katrakis, we are going to move you to a more comfortable space."

"Okay," she said.

But she looked vacant. Like she was only half there.

He lingered behind as she was wheeled away, and took out his phone. He called his PA. "Cancel my meetings for the next week. There is a pressing matter I must take care of."

He had hired Carla primarily because she was an old dragon who yelled at him when she disapproved of him, and gave him a strange sort of structure neither of his parents had ever managed. His mother had ignored him, his father had beaten him. Carla was a happy medium.

Predictably, she sighed. "Does that mean you're going on a bender?"

He looked around at the sterile space. "Yes. I am terribly sorry, but I currently have two supermodels ready to climb into my limo, and then into my bed. And I am not planning on curbing the adventure until it curbs itself."

"You're lucky that you're charming," she said. "Otherwise there's no way you could have conned investors into throwing money at a business the owner is never in the office of."

"I guess I am very lucky."

He hung up, and made his way to the recovery area that she was being installed in. He wasn't going to leave until she was discharged. He had done little for his brother in the last few years. And the feeling of failure was intense.

He could do this. He could stay with Ariadne.

And he would.

It was like a spa. Except here her grief had been compounded. Here, everything really did feel like it was crumbling around her.

The room she was staying in had a glorious whirlpool tub, but when she got into it, and let the hot water soothe her, it was soothing away lingering cramps. And the cramps were a reminder. A reminder of her loss.

A reminder that she had failed. She had failed this baby.

She hadn't ever wanted to hurt like this. Who did? But Ariadne had taken so many steps to try and avoid ever feeling pain.

As a child, she'd been like another suitcase her father had to bring any time he moved. Nothing more. Like his luggage, she would appear in his new home and then get packed away again. He was invested in his relationships.

His tempestuous love affairs and marriages were so much more interesting than the little girl he'd been left with when his first marriage dissolved. Though at least he had made sure she had a place to stay, she supposed.

Her mother had simply gone away, and Ariadne had never even missed her. Because how could you miss a vapor that had never played a substantial role in your life?

She'd vowed to be a different kind of mother. It was one of the gifts she'd known her marriage would bring. Children. Children she could love and cherish. Could be there for so they weren't lonely like she'd been.

Theseus had wanted to wait to have children. They had always planned on using artificial insemination. They didn't have an intimate marriage, and there was no reason, with the advent of modern medicine that they had to. She wanted to rage at him now about so many things. About not doing this sooner. About not freezing embryos or banking more sperm. About not…

Not staying here with her.

He was gone. He was gone and it wasn't fair.

It was like an aching, endless pit inside of her.

Her grief might not be what everybody thought it was, but it was deep.

He was the closest friend that she had in the world. Her most constant companion.

He was gone and so was her hope. This child had been her hope. Of being happy again. Of loving again. Of having a future that didn't feel cold and dark and sad.

She picked her phone up and looked at her texts. James had sent her something and…she was going to have to tell him. She couldn't, not right now, not while things were so raw and awful.

Not while they were still tentative—with Patrocles and the inheritance.

It wasn't for her. It was for the employees. For Theseus. For James, even.

She heard footsteps in the corridor, as if the universe was reminding her that she was in fact not alone at all. Because Dionysus had not left since he had brought her here two days ago.

She set her phone back down.

"I really hate to be the one to get in the way of your preferred lifestyle," she said.

He had barely made it to Dionysus's funeral. He had rolled in hungover, and he had left with a woman on his arm.

"Believe me when I tell you, nothing gets in the way if I don't want it to. You need someone to stay with you."

"Supporting your brother a little bit late?"

That wasn't fair. His jaw went tight.

She didn't need her complicated Dionysus feelings rising to the fore right now.

Things were complicated enough.

"I'm sorry," he said. "Sorry that I… I wasn't as close with him these past years as I might have been."

Of course they hadn't been close. It had been a tangle of lies, and Dionysus didn't even know that. But how could he be close to them?

When their marriage wasn't what it seemed. When the fight they'd had at the engagement party all those years ago wasn't about what he believed it to be.

If Dionysus knew the truth, maybe he would understand. But if Dionysus knew the truth, it would…it could undermine what Theseus had deferred his own happiness and freedom to achieve and she just wouldn't do that.

She stood up, and walked out onto the terrace. It overlooked a beautiful courtyard with fruit trees, well-manicured pathways and perfect hedgerows. So beautiful it nearly felt like a mockery. She could see cars driving beyond all this, in the distance. Life carried on.

She wanted to stop time for a moment.

"I imagine you've spoken to your father about this?"

"No," he said. "Why would I do that?"

"Because he has to know eventually. And he'll decide I suppose if he's going to give the company to you or to himself."

"I have not told my father. And everybody here is under strict orders to keep things completely silent."

"But surely at work…"

"I called. I made excuses. I said that you needed some time away to grieve."

"I didn't take any time away as it happened."

"Grief is strange. It can become more intense with time. Once the shock wears away. At least, I've heard."

She turned back and looked at him speculatively. Was he talking about himself? It was so impossible to tell with him. But she knew that he wasn't unfeeling. She had known him long enough to know that he was someone who felt very deeply. At least, he had at one time. She could remember his moods, his temper, his declarations that some food or another was the best he had ever had, or that a sunset was the most beautiful.

It had changed, as he had begun to channel that into more physical pursuits. But she felt like it had to be a part of him still. Somewhere.

Which meant his grief for Theseus must be raw.

"Thank you."

The breeze caught her hair, and she closed her eyes, trying to let go. Trying to let go of the dream that she had just lost. She visualized it. She couldn't.

If you think about it, I am a piece of my brother out in the world.

She stilled. Everything in her suddenly alight. She turned and looked at Dionysus. "You are identical."

"You only recently told me that we were not."

"Not me, maybe. But genetically, you are identical."

"Yes," he said. "That is how identical twins work. We are the copy paste of the natural world."

"That means that a DNA test would not be able to determine whether a child was Theseus's or yours." Her heart started to beat harder. Faster. "Dionysus," she said. "I need to have your baby."

CHAPTER THREE

DIONYSUS LIVED HIS life in such a way that very few things had the power to shock him. But this succeeded.

Ariadne succeeded.

Wasn't that the story of his existence? Ariadne got beneath his skin where no one else ever could.

"And how exactly would that be accomplished?"

He had an idea. One that was vivid, and blasphemous given the circumstances. Given that his brother had only been dead in the ground for two weeks.

Given that she was his sister-in-law.

That she was as forbidden to him now as she had ever been.

Given that she was now frail and recovering from what had just happened.

"Insemination," she said.

His lip curled. "You expect that I will… Go into a clinical bathroom and take myself in hand."

"Of course not, you idiot. You're a billionaire. Use your imagination. You will go into your luxury bedroom and take yourself in hand."

She made eye contact with him, her expression bold,

her cheeks bright red, indicating that she was not quite so unbothered by the image as she was pretending to be.

That was Ariadne.

It had always shocked him that she had been quite so infatuated with Theseus.

Dionysus loved his brother, but there was so much seriousness in him. He never had the fight that Dionysus did. He didn't carry the rage.

In the end, Dionysus often felt that it was the rage which kept him going. The rage which compelled him on when it sometimes felt as if things were hopeless.

It was also likely what had kept him and Ariadne apart. There was an intensity there that vibrated with far too much energy.

Theseus had been easy for her to get close to because of his stillness.

Though then, Ariadne had been bold.

He could remember her well as a young girl running feral about the island. When they first met, he would never have known that she was the daughter of a wealthy family who had their house built across the sandy expanse of shore. He would have imagined that she was the daughter of a cook, or perhaps a stable hand.

Their father took far too much of an interest in everything they did. He ruled them with an iron fist. Ariadne's father, by contrast, barely seemed to remember that he had a daughter. She had been raised by a series of nannies, and as she had gotten older, by no one at all.

A girl isolated and lonely in a palatial estate. Theseus and Dionysus had adopted her with vigor.

She had climbed rocks barefoot, leapt from waterfalls into deep clear pools below. Her dark hair had always been a mass of tangles.

After she had married Theseus, she had changed. They didn't have the closeness they'd had as boys, but he and Theseus had still spent holidays together, and of course both were members of the Diamond Club, as the richest pair of twins in the world.

And two of the richest men on earth in their own right.

They also often attended many of the same charity events. Where Ariadne tamed all her wildness and presented herself as a sleek socialite.

But this, this right here was the fire that he expected to see in her eyes. This was the intensity that he counted on from Ariadne. At least the Ariadne of old. Problem solving, never letting go. Clinging to something with all tenacity.

He had seen glimpses of this woman over the years. Flashes of the wild thing she'd been once and he'd always wanted to draw her all the way to the surface.

He could remember baiting her at the last gala they'd both been at.

The girl I knew once would have dared me to steal a bottle of champagne and swim in the fountain.

The girl you knew once didn't have responsibilities.

A shame then, that we've both had to grow up.

We don't live in Neverland.

A painful thought since he could have easily seen the two of them as Wendy and Peter. Perhaps he was more Captain Hook.

But now the girl with fire in her eyes was back.

He should hate that it was due to her loss. He found it hard to hate anything about the sparks in her eyes.

Her request was as a predator, tearing through his chest.

"You would have me be… A favorite uncle? To my own child?" he asked.

"Yes," she said, her tone placid. "You don't want children, do you?"

"No," he said. Simply.

If there had been a notion in him to carry on his bloodline, if he had even for a second of time entertained that he might marry, find a wife, produce children, he had given it up long ago. And he would not allow it to be revived now.

Not during this discussion. This discussion of him providing *his brother* with the heir he could no longer have.

With the woman who had been haunting his dreams since he was a boy.

"Then why should it be a problem?" she asked. "Many people donate their genetic material toward the creation of a child, it does not make them that child's mother or father. My mother, for instance, was certainly never around."

"No indeed," he said. "But a noted difference is that I would be in the child's life. Presumably. And that might complicate things."

"Is that a bad thing? Fatherhood, in a sense, without the real responsibility of it?"

She believed what the press said about him. That much was clear. She no longer saw him as the boy she'd known when they'd spent their days running free in the forest. She thought he'd become the kind of man who could father a child and pretend it hadn't happened.

The media painted his portrait in that shape. He had never minded it.

He minded it now.

"And what will you tell the child?" he asked.

She looked stunned by that. "The child has yet to come into existence, so I think I have time to figure that out."

"And what will your story be? Because you have lost this baby, which I assume must have been nearly a month along." His words sounded flat and calloused even to his own ears.

"Timing?" She blinked. "That's what you're concerned about?"

"It is not wrong to concern myself with the credibility of this."

"I will tell your father that Theseus banked his sperm. In case there were issues."

"All right." He had to admit that was possible. A man in Theseus's position would likely have put something like that in place. In fact, he was surprised his brother hadn't.

"So you'll admit that you lost a pregnancy, but claim you had artificial insemination done afterward."

"*If* questions of timing arise. And if they do, undoubtedly at that point your father will demand a DNA test. Which I will give. And it will be impossible to tell whether or not the child was fathered by you or by Theseus. And in fact, doing so would demand… I believe it's extensive genetic sequencing, which can no longer be done on your brother, since he is deceased." She swallowed hard. "I know. This is all extremely hard and mercenary. When Theseus is dead, and my baby is lost. I don't feel mercenary about it. I don't feel hard. But I cannot allow this to break me. And I cannot allow your father to win. One thing I need you to understand, is that Theseus hated your father."

That shocked him. To his core. Because as far as Dionysus was concerned, Theseus was their father's puppet. It was nearly impossible to imagine that his brother who had behaved as a performing monkey for their father all this time *hated* the man.

He knew they'd both…had complicated relationships with him but Theseus's willingness to please him had convinced Dionysus it was a Stockholm Syndrome situation.

He wasn't a psychologist but he knew well enough just how complicated things were with abusive parents.

"He never indicated as much to me."

"He wouldn't have. It was important that he kept that secret. Under control. Because he never wanted to lose his power over the shipping company. He worked to change things. You have no idea the state it was in when he took over."

"Why didn't he publicize that it was in poor condition?"

"It wasn't the company. It was the treatment of its employees. It was workplace safety. Wages. There were so many illegal things happening, and he restructured it all. He changed people's lives. Your brother was a very good man. And you might be angry at him for leaving. I know that I am sometimes. But he was a man who cared very deeply about all of these things, and it was a weight that he carried that grew heavier and heavier as time went on. One thing I know for sure is that I cannot allow your father to put his hand back into this company. I have to preserve it. I have to save it. And I want Theseus to have a legacy. That legacy will be a child that grows up to be nothing like your father. That legacy will be a child who has a father that he can be proud of, even if he isn't here."

"And for yourself?"

"Of course I'm…" She suddenly looked very small and lost. "I can't think about myself right now. Because I've lost too much. Because if I start to ponder the intensity of everything that is now gone for me I'm afraid that I'm going to collapse. I won't be able to stand back up. I can't afford it. Not right now. All I can do is keep moving forward. So will you do this for me or not?"

That actually was no choice to be made. He hated it. The very idea of it all. But…

Hearing what his brother had been carrying, work that he had done, and feeling the extreme guilt he did over not being closer to his brother these past years when their time had been limited, what else could he do?

He owed his brother. It was as simple as that. Though he would not give her confirmation just yet.

"We will need to come to an agreement on details."

"Good. I'll talk to the doctor about…" Her eyes filled with tears. "When will be best to proceed." She was so strong, even as she sat there looking devastated. Her dark hair reminded him more now of the girl she had been. No longer captured in a smooth bun, but wild curls framing her face, falling down her back.

She was pale. Strong.

She had always been slender, and petite. And always containing an immense amount of strength. Much more than you would have ever imagined a girl her size could carry. Now a woman with slender shoulders carrying the weight of his brother's legacy.

Foregoing any thought to her own.

"Your safety is paramount," he said. "I will not allow you to sacrifice yourself upon the altar of my brother's legacy. I need to know if you're at a greater risk of hemorrhage than another woman might be. Do you understand me?"

She looked at him. "And why exactly should you have anything to say about that?"

"Because my brother appears to have sacrificed himself upon the legacy of our company. And I think it's quite enough martyring for one family, don't you?"

"It isn't martyring. It is simply doing the right thing. I know that that's antithetical to your libertine lifestyle."

"There is more than one way to throw yourself onto a pyre, Ariadne. Of this I am certain. But there isn't any reason for you to continue doing it."

"I want a child," she said, her voice getting thin. "I was… You know about my childhood. I was very lonely. My parents barely acknowledged that I existed. They still barely acknowledge my existence. And you know that. I want to be the kind of mother that I never had. That I never saw. I don't want to have a child simply for the legacy. I want to have a child so that I can love them. And if I can't have this baby, not only will I lose the staff that has become so important to me, this company that has become part of my own legacy, part of something that I have built, I will lose the future that I was planning for myself. I will be left entirely alone. Theseus was my best friend. He was my confidant. He was the person I was closest to in all of this world. And he's gone. I can't call him and speak to him. I cannot say good morning to him. I cannot seek shelter in his arms as I try to figure out how to deal with both his loss and the loss of our child."

"And I'm very sorry," he said, hot emotion rising up in his chest. "But I am not the one who took anything from you."

"I know that. But I just hope, that because of the love you have for your brother, and because of the friendship that you and I have shared for so long, that you will... Take that into account as you make your decision."

"If you fall pregnant, you will come and stay with me. I will not allow you to be by yourself. Not after that."

"You're never home," she pointed out.

"Then I will be."

"Don't get controlling," she said.

"Is it controlling when you are an integral part of something?"

It was not a question. He would rearrange everything to make sure that Ariadne was safe. There were spare few people in his life that mattered to him. She was one of them. His brother had been the other.

She was right to say that it was his feelings for the both of them that compelled him now.

Her doctor came in after and told her that she was free to leave today. And he took it upon himself to make arrangements to get them both out of England as quickly and discreetly as possible. His private jet was outfitted and ready to go, and he had decided that he knew exactly what they needed.

She was correct, of course. They would not be conducting this pregnancy attempt in a standard clinic. They had the luxury of bringing the perfect team to them, and he fully expected to take advantage of that. Not that he knew anything about trying to help a woman get pregnant. His expertise lay in the prevention thereof, if anything.

But he intended to become an expert, and quickly.

"Are we headed back to my town house or…" she asked once they were on the road, being driven toward the airport, and, quite clearly not toward her town house.

"No," he said.

"Didn't I tell you not to get controlling?"

"You also asked for my sperm. I feel like we're living in a strange time where our boundaries are not quite as clear as they used to be."

"Dionysus…"

"We are going to Greece," he said. He paused for a moment, feeling like he was about to peel back the curtains covering his deepest heart and expose things he'd rather not. "I bought the island, you know."

She looked at him, shocked. "No. I didn't know that. Why would I know that?"

The realization she hadn't known hollowed out a space inside of him.

"I thought perhaps Theseus might've told you."

"Theseus didn't speak of that island."

"A shame then. Because there were good times there too."

"Maybe for you. Your father was hideous to him. He was—"

"Our father was with us whether we were on that island or not. Our father was with us always." He tapped on his temple. "Our father's greatest game was being in our minds. Don't you think that is true? Our father's words were the poison in his veins then. Telling him that he had no value. Telling him that he would never be good enough. Don't you agree?"

He watched as she swallowed hard. "I suppose so."

"You know it to be true. Perhaps he felt a certain measure of trauma tied to the island, but I don't. I consider it taking control back. Anyway, if I was happy anywhere, it was there."

It was perhaps a little bit more revealing than he had intended it to be. He hadn't realized until he had said the words just how true they were. He had loved his time on the island, because it was where they had met Ariadne. Because it was the only place they ever had any freedom. When they were in England they were locked away in a manor house with teachers dictating their every movement. When they were in Athens it was the same. Their father's corporation had always maintained offices in both countries, and that meant they spent a significant amount of time in both. Their father was Greek in heritage, but often more English in nationality. Their mother had been English.

Still, it had been essential that they spoke Greek.

Spanish. Japanese. Chinese. Part of their rigorous education to make them superhuman. Men without flaws.

Of course, it had been an asset to Dionysus in business. And also in pleasure. Though he found words were often unnecessary when he seduced a woman, it was nice to be able to communicate at least on a rudimentary level. And the removal of language barriers certainly made things more interesting.

Dionysus wasn't certain if his father really cared about his sons being a glorious reflection of him, or if he simply liked to flex control when and as he could. And having control over their education down to the very last detail was having control over them.

Having control over their minds, as he had just said.

"I was happy on the island," Ariadne said softly.

He was surprised to hear her say that, if only because the weight of his transgression loomed large between them without Theseus here. He felt no guilt over it. He had wanted her and it had been his one chance to taste her.

He regretted that he'd damaged his closeness with his brother.

But he *never* regretted that he'd kissed her.

"I won't mind going there," she continued.

But she hadn't, he realized. Because Theseus hadn't wanted to. Theseus had known Dionysus had bought the island. He'd known about his plans for it. They had spoken about it over drinks at the Diamond Club only last year.

He had invited them to come, and Theseus had not said anything half so bold as *I hate it there*. He had been as he ever was. Diplomatic. Easy.

He had said that of course when they were able to clear their schedules both he and Ariadne would be delighted to come to the island.

But they never had. And he had decided for some reason that Ariadne was the one who did not wish to go. Perhaps because he often tied pain in his chest to Ariadne. If he tied it to his brother, if he blamed Theseus, well, that would have been a loss he couldn't afford. He had never wanted to cut ties with his twin.

And now his twin was gone.

They pulled into the section of the airport which housed private aircraft. They were taken right to his jet. They got out of the car and he braced her.

"I'm all right," she said.

"I don't wish for you to fall. You still seem fragile."

She looked up at him, green eyes sparkling. "Does anything about me seem fragile?"

No. In spite of her frame, she had never seemed fragile. That was why it had been so terrifying to watch her fold like that in the club. To glimpse her mortality.

It all felt too raw. Too frightening. He trusted nothing. The world was cruel. It always had been. But it seemed eager to flex that cruelty now in a way that it had not for the past several decades.

"Is my father's house still there?" she asked as they boarded the plane.

"No," he said. "Both homes were leveled. I cleared them out. Built one new residence for myself. There is nothing and no one else on the island."

She looked shocked. "Really?"

"I always thought the perfect paradise would have been one without our families there. One where we were allowed to roam free and wild. I suppose I made that for myself."

"And you have massive parties there every weekend?"

"No," he said gravely. "I don't."

She looked baffled by that.

"But I would have thought…"

Anger rose up inside him, and he did not bother to hold it back.

"Do you know me, Ariadne, or do you only know now what the papers print about me?"

He didn't know why it irritated him, that she had reduced him to the headlines, the same as everybody else.

It wasn't that they weren't true, they were. He was an incorrigible libertine. All the better to numb life's pain. All the better to manage his rage.

Rage that had knit his bones together in the womb, a legacy from his father. Twisted by his upbringing.

Cemented when he'd lost the one woman he'd ever cared about.

He had changed.

But he was also still *himself*. He was still the boy that she had known. He still found solace in remote and wild places. In swimming beneath natural waterfalls and lying in the sand. He still found sanity in olive groves and solitude. He was not only the voracious monster that devoured everything in his path. Turning it all to hedonistic pleasure.

It was not *all* he was.

She was the only person left on earth who ought to know that.

He wondered then, how Theseus had spoken of him, in the privacy of their home. Because he had seemed as pleasant as ever the last time they'd seen each other, but surely, Theseus's own vision of him must have shaped hers.

"What am I supposed to think? We haven't been *close* in years, and you know that. Small talk at events and holiday dinners packed full of other business associates is hardly a relationship. It isn't as if we… Talk the way that we used to. We are not children. We have lives. You went out and started a major company, and I do applaud you for that. The success that you have, you earned yourself, and it is an amazing thing. Different, and no less amazing, was Theseus taking that empire that was rotten to the core and turning it into something that he could be proud of. But you know that there has been distance these past years. You know that. We see each other, we talk as if we are still friends. We smile. But I don't know anything about your life beyond what I read. You banter with me, you don't *talk* to me. It's different." She settled onto the leather sofa in the main portion of the private plane. And he took his seat in the chair across from her.

"Is that what you think? That I have become a stranger to you now?"

"Tell me about your life. Prove me wrong."

"Perhaps you should tell me about yours too." Because he had to question what he really knew about her life. He saw her socially, along with his brother, but right now with the loss of Theseus looming large he felt the true gap between them. The real distance.

"You first," she said.

"I'm one of the richest men in the world."

"I know," she said, her tone flat. "We're in a club dedicated to that. That is a Wikipedia entry. It isn't you. If you want me to know more than I can read on the Internet, then give me more."

He cycled through everything he had done in the past year. Finished the rebuilding of the island, that was the main thing. It was one thing that nobody knew about, likely because it wasn't interesting, and didn't further his image in the media as a break. Everybody liked to keep to their particular narratives.

It wasn't a secret, it was only that it wasn't interesting.

That was why there were no stories about it.

Then there was travel. Every city he was in a blur. Business meetings. What was there to say? That was what he didn't understand.

They had once talked about dreams. But he was in

the middle of living those dreams, wasn't he? So what was there to say?

"Tell me about a typical day for you," she said.

"And how is that not some pithy newspaper interview?"

"It isn't," she said. "Because I want you to give me an honest answer, not one that would make a good pull quote."

"All right," he said. "I wake up around noon, and begin the day."

"I don't believe that."

"Why don't you believe it?"

"Because you run a successful billion-dollar business. And I find it very hard to believe that you're accomplishing that waking up so late."

"It is a global business. And that means that I'm working across time zones. It means I don't have to rise early."

That was true.

"All right. So you're a night owl. You were always like that. I remember I used to go down to the beach late and find you there."

He jerked away from her, the memory too sharp.

"Yes," he said.

"Go on."

"I have very strong coffee, ignore the hangover, begin having business meetings. I work until around nine, and then it is time to go out. Of course, going out is often tied to work. There are specific clubs and venues that I visit in order to forge relationships with investors, and partner with businesses. That shouldn't surprise you. Now the sex, that has nothing to do with business."

He watched her face. It went pink.

"Great. Thank you for sharing."

"I had thought that you might want honesty," he said.

"Of course. Nothing is more important than honesty."

"I think that you are being sarcastic. But this is what you asked for."

"I thought maybe you might tell me about a relationship that you had in the last year."

"A one-night stand is not a relationship, and I realize that you may not know that, since even my brother married very young. But there is nothing to say. I don't know their names. And if I do, I forget them soon after."

"That's what doesn't seem like you."

He lifted a brow. "How?" What he hated was that he cared about the answer. That he cared what she thought about him. That he cared whether or not she had seen this in him when he was a boy.

He shouldn't.

Because he had refashioned himself into something new, something stronger, something insulated from all of the emotions that he'd once had, as he'd needed to do it to survive. To move beyond the abuse that he had suffered at the hands of his father. To move beyond the way that Ariadne had…

"Because you used to care. You would never have treated people like they were interchangeable or disposable. Yes, you were reckless. But with yourself. Not with others. That is the part that makes you a stranger to me. It is the thing that makes me question whether or not you… I don't know what happened to you. And this is why we don't know each other. Because you pulled away from people. From us."

Anger spiked in his veins. She wasn't going to acknowledge it. And if not, then he would.

"Here's another Wikipedia entry for you, Ariadne. Ten years ago on a balcony, on my future sister-in-law's eighteenth birthday, I took her in my arms and kissed her. She kissed me back because she thought I was my brother, and I didn't care."

Her face went scarlet. "You *knew* that I thought you were Theseus."

"So you said at the time. And yet you say I've changed? If you always believed that of me, then you never truly thought me any better than this, did you?"

"We agreed to leave that in the past," she said. "I know Theseus forgave you. I did too. But you were never as close to us…"

Rage was his constant companion. Low level static in the background of his soul. Normally, keeping hold of it was easy.

But she was asking him to give her a baby. And at the same time scolding him for the way he'd carved out a life for himself. Especially when she'd believed the worst in him when he'd believed them to be friends. He would not mind if not for the naked hypocrisy of it.

"*I* wasn't? The two of you concealed yourself in that estate of yours in London. You were completely inaccessible to the outside world. There are no photos of you that are not carefully crafted to project a certain image. You don't simply go out, you go and perform. How dare you accuse me of changing? How dare you accuse me of performing for headlines or being somehow inauthentic when you and Theseus were strangers to me every time I ever saw a picture of you. I'm convinced it's why my brother called me as little as possible. Because he never wanted to have a discussion about it. Because he never wished to be called out on the fact that he was… Engaging in some masquerade for all the world to see. And for some reason you were involved in that. For some reason, the most honest, feral, forthright girl I had ever known became a woman who lived behind a mask. Perhaps explain that to me."

"Because we had a legacy. Because we were trying to repair things."

"To protect my father?"

"No. To protect Theseus. Because you know that your father would have wrenched everything back if for one moment he had been disappointed in Theseus's life. If he had been disappointed in the profits that the company was putting out. If he thought that Theseus was in there intentionally dismantling the system that your father had put in place. It was a tightrope walk. I know this is difficult for you to understand Dionysus, but sometimes people do things and it isn't about you. In fact, we didn't think of you at all."

He was past feeling wounded by such things.

"I am well aware that you didn't think of me, Ariadne. There is no need for you to draw a line beneath it."

Her rage was a living thing. Palpable.

Good. She should be angry. She should think about what he had said. He could understand that his brother was living in a different reality, but...

You shut them out as well, you know that.

Of course Theseus had said the kiss was forgotten. Forgiven. But they'd never been the same after. The twin bond, strong though they were so different, had fractured that night and it had never, ever been the same.

At the time, Dionysus hadn't even wanted it to be. He'd wanted Theseus to be scorched as he was.

"Maybe the simple truth is you don't want to know who I am now," she said. "And maybe I don't want to know you."

"Good thing then, that we don't have to in order to have a child together. Especially one that I can never claim."

"Of course we don't. There is nothing intimate about artificial insemination."

"You say that as if you know."

Her head jerked away, and she looked out the window. Her stock response to that surprised him. And it made him wonder.

But there was no reason that she and his brother would have used insemination. Unless they had trouble getting pregnant. In which case, his comments were likely very insensitive.

But that was fine. She was so disgusted with who he was now. She could be disgusted with his lack of sensitivity too.

All fine with him.

"I'm tired," she said. "I think I'll go lie down before we arrive in Greece."

"Yes. Get your rest."

And when she abandoned him to walk into the private bedroom on the plane, he found himself letting out a breath he had not been aware he'd been keeping in. Likely since she had collapsed in the club.

Nothing with Ariadne would ever be simple.

But he was committed to behaving as if it were.

Because what was the point of a well-crafted façade if it abandoned him when he needed it most?

No. He would do this for her. This favor. He would use it to wipe his conscience clean. And then...

He would forget Ariadne and the child existed.

He would have to.

CHAPTER FOUR

ARIADNE WOKE UP as the plane began its descent.

She was groggy, and fragile—in spite of what she'd said to Dionysus. Everything hurt. Her heart, and her body.

She was still in disbelief that she had asked Dionysus to father her baby. And in even greater disbelief that he had agreed. And that they were on their way back to this island where they had once been children. Where things had been simple. When they had not fought with each other, or played games.

Until they had.

She was still dressed in her clothes from yesterday, and she tried to smooth the creases out of them as she exited the bedroom, and went back into the sitting area. Dionysus was still seated in that chair. Or rather, he was back in it. There was something mysterious and powerful, she thought, in the way he maintained the exact same posture as he had when she had left.

It was by design, she was nearly certain. Because that was him.

It struck her then, the truth of that. He had curated

MILLIE ADAMS 57

an image. He might be angry at her for believing the press, but who had informed the press of who he was. He had. Dionysus was not a fool. Every asset he had to his name bore witness to that truth. He had built his company from the ground up. His father's name was a blight, if anything. And yet, he had styled himself a billionaire, one of the richest men in the world. A member of the Diamond Club.

She was as well, but her entry was a collaborative effort. The same could not be said for Dionysus.

She knew exactly why Theseus had crafted an image and clung to it so dearly. She had her own opinions on whether the extent of it was necessary, but his own trauma was wrapped so tightly around his costume, the adhesive of bandages he wrapped around his wounds firmly affixing the mask to his face. She might have disagreed with that, but she did not know how to tell him it was wrong. Perhaps she should have. Yes, in hindsight, she questioned if the cost had not been worth the promised reward.

Of course there had been happiness. But it had been had in secret.

Both of them had been the staid, lovely power couple in public. Only in private did they laugh. Share secrets and stories.

Only in private could Theseus love and be loved.

She swallowed hard. "I slept well."

She moved to the couch she had been seated on prior to taking her leave.

"Good," he said, sounding supremely unconcerned either way.

"Somehow I don't think you mean that."

"I would rather have you well rested. Especially given the state of things."

"My fragility?"

"You find that word so offensive. Why?"

He was looking at her, his eyes far too keen.

"You are one of the richest men in the world," she said, doing her level best to continue to meet his challenging gaze. "But there is always something a person can't afford. No matter how wealthy."

"Is that true?"

"Yes. I cannot afford to be fragile. I have to keep moving. For some reason, Dionysus, I think that you believe you can't afford to care."

She was rewarded by a lift of his brow.

He really was astonishing to look at. She marveled at the ways in which he and Theseus were identical, and yet not. Not to her.

They never had been. Right at first, she had struggled to tell them apart. Though she had noticed quickly that Dionysus had a small scar at the bottom of his chin. The light in his eyes was different. The mischief.

Where Theseus always seemed burdened by an invisible weight, Dionysus seemed to always be fencing with an invisible enemy. And that, she realized in the moment was the difference between the two brothers' burdens.

What Theseus had tried to carry, Dionysus chose to do battle with.

"You know me so well," he said.

"I did once."

"Yes. Once." They were silent for the rest of the descent, and she looked out the window, at the familiar white sand they approached. At the crystal blue water.

Her heart began to race. She hadn't been back here since she was a teenager.

Her father had sold his home shortly after she had married Theseus, and shortly before his sixth divorce. She wasn't sure where all the homes he owned were now. He had come to Theseus's funeral, a new wife on his arm, of course. But he had not... They had never checked in on her.

She didn't need him. Even now, she didn't need him.

The landing was smooth, and she could only attribute the dread in her stomach to the memories here.

The memories were good, in part. But they were twisted around the pain of her childhood. And now around the loss of the man who had been such an integral piece of these years.

But Dionysus remained.

So when he stood and reached out his hand, she took it.

They disembarked from the plane, and the hot wind coming in from the Groves touched her skin, reviving something in her after all the damp of London.

She hadn't left England in the past year. All of her

global meetings had been done via the computer. As she had tried to prepare for pregnancy, as she had worked at the company, as she had done her best to try and manage the life they had built, the façade that was so important to them both, she had found herself increasingly isolated and stagnant. She hadn't fully realized it until just now.

She closed her eyes, and let the familiar air kiss her face.

Theseus might be gone, but the island greeted her as an old friend. And she found it did not feel so empty or lost as she had expected it to.

A tear slid down her cheek.

"Are you well?"

She turned and looked at Dionysus, and she was thrown backward. Into a memory. Or maybe not even a specific memory. But the feeling of a moment. Of running with him along the banks of their favorite swimming hole. Him grabbing her hand and pulling her in with him.

She could remember well the frame of his wiry, strong body.

Her throat ached.

She could remember his smile.

Sneaking strawberry cake and champagne.

And the moment he'd found her on a darkened balcony and taken her into his arms.

It might not be a singular moment. But a hundred pieced together.

And it was no less powerful for that. Perhaps, it was even more.

"I didn't expect to be... So happy to be back."

Another tear slid down her cheek. He reached out, and brushed his thumb over her cheekbone, capturing one of her tears. His hand was rough.

She wondered why. All she could do was stare at him, look into those dark eyes. Not familiar because they were the same shape and color as her late husband's. Because he was Dionysus. And he had once been as familiar to her as breathing. As the air here. As the feeling of the sun on her skin.

She swallowed hard, and moved away from him, breaking the contact of his touch.

"Where's the new house?"

"I will drive us there. I have a car just here."

He gestured to the garage that was nearly hidden by the side of a rock. The door slid open as they approached, and inside was a bright red sports car that was as unsubtle as its owner. And she would love to be scathing about that. She would love, absolutely, to tie that to the new, hedonistic version of Dionysus who had changed so much since their childhood. But this... This was him. In fact...

"This looks very like the car that you had when you were seventeen. I remember you sending me a photo of it."

"It is in fact the car that I had when I was seventeen,"

he said, grinning. "I could think of no better vehicle to serve me on the island."

It was such a strange, nostalgic sort of thing. But then, the entire purchase of the island was such a nostalgic thing for a man who seemed to fashion his life around the entire concept that he cared for nothing and no one.

It disrupted her thoughts on him. She wasn't in the mood to be disrupted. Not right now.

So she got into the car without thinking too deeply about any of it, and let him drive them both up a new road that had been cut into the island. His new house must not be on the beach.

She couldn't see where it was. The road was winding, and the grounds were no longer manicured in any fashion. It was like the island had taken control back.

And then, she could see windows, glinting through the trees. A house made of dark natural stone cut into hard angles seemingly set into the rock. It was entirely different to the ostentatious and palatial dwellings their families had had on the island.

This seemed designed to complement the surrounding environment, rather than take it over.

There was a staircase that led up to the front door, because the house was indeed seemingly melted to the side of the mountain.

"Part of the house extends back into the rock," he said. "It's very effective for cooling. And helps reduce some of the carbon footprint."

"Oh," she said.

It was a very stupid thing to say. It wasn't crisp or charged. It wasn't pithy or clever.

But she found she couldn't make fun of him for caring about something. Whether that was the environment or anything.

In some ways, she supposed he was demonstrating care in a fashion by bringing her here.

Even though she had been annoyed with him for taking her out of her life.

The trouble was, she wasn't sure what her life was at the moment.

As she and Dionysus got out of the car, she looked at him. And realized that for the foreseeable future, he was her life.

He was going to be the father of her baby.

She felt like the wind had been knocked out of her in one great gust.

Dionysus was going to be the father of her baby. And it was easy enough for her to lean on the fact that genetically, the child would be indistinguishable from a baby that she and Theseus had made.

But it was different. It was simply different.

Theseus was her friend. The idea of having his baby, a baby that was part of both of them, had felt like the ultimate expression of their friendship. The way they'd melded their lives together. It hadn't been a conventional partnership, but it had been real. The thought of carrying his baby had not been… *Intimate*.

What a strange word. As she stood there staring at Dionysus's proud profile, the idea of his child growing in her womb felt...

It made goose bumps raise on her arms.

And she had another memory. Of when they had been young. Still teenagers. Treading water in the middle of that swimming hole. And his eyes had gone dark when he had looked at her, and when his gaze had flickered down to her mouth, she had panicked.

Because she had made a promise.

She had made a promise to Theseus, and she couldn't betray that promise.

Because she had known in that moment that if she drew closer to Dionysus, everything would be ruined.

She didn't want passion. She wanted to be cared for while caring for someone else. She wanted companionship.

She wanted stability.

She had watched her father discard women, one after the other all through her life. When they got too mouthy, too bored, too old. Passion was fleeting and selfish. She did not want to live a life governed by passion.

She had decided instead on a life without it entirely.

She loved Theseus. With her entire soul.

But Dionysus had begun calling to that wild thing within her she tried so hard to keep hidden, and when he'd kissed her on the balcony...

Of course she'd told Theseus she had thought it was him.

She wasn't sure either of them believed her.

But she'd done her best to forget it all. To put it behind her. Still…

He was Dionysus.

The only reason she hadn't felt his impact like a wrecking ball when she had seen him in the Diamond Club was that she had been in a state of shock for the past two weeks. And then she had miscarried.

Her body was wrapped in discomfort and sadness.

But right now, she didn't feel as if she had the protection of those horrible feelings. Right now, she was left with the impact of him. And memories. And honesty.

About the real reason she didn't like seeing him as much as she once had. About the real reasons the headlines about his exploits bothered her.

Yes. Right then, she was confronted with honesty, and she hated that most of all.

When he turned to face her, it was like seeing him for the first time. The sun hit the side of his face, casting a harsh light on his strong features. That proud nose, his sensual lips. His square jaw. The slight dip in his chin, a scar, not a feature. Because it was the one physical feature on his face that differed from Theseus.

And yet it was an entirely different face. The sight of it did entirely different things to her body.

Where Theseus was home and comfort, love, if faded from a red rose to a yellow one as the years had passed, Dionysus was a straight shot of whiskey.

And there was nothing comfortable about him.

There never had been.

She didn't like these feelings, because they reminded her of being seventeen. And torn violently between two truths. One being that she loved Theseus as much as she could have ever loved anyone.

And the other, she had been increasingly confronted by the pull she felt to Dionysus that was nothing like the affectionate feelings she had for his brother.

But she had made a vow when she was fifteen. To keep Theseus's secret. To marry him.

She could remember that so clearly. They had been out on the beach too late, and he had sat so close to her on the sand. And part of her had wondered if he would finally tell her that he had feelings for her like she did for him. What had come was a sobbing confession she hadn't expected. She had ended up holding him in her arms while he told her that he had tried to ignore his feelings all of his life, but recently had had a romance with the son of one of the visitors to the island, and he couldn't deny it any longer.

He was gay and he was never going to be what their father wanted him to be.

I fear he might actually kill me.

He won't. I'll protect you.

Will you? You are my dearest friend in the world. And I love you. If you marry me... If we can have children, then I can be what my father needs me to be. And he never has to know. No one ever has to know.

She had agreed. Because she had been young, and she had loved him.

And it had been a sharp, uncomfortable thing.

By the time she married him, she had known it was never going to be romantic. Those were a foolish teenage girl's hopes and dreams. But she had accepted that in the way Theseus had given up on the idea of truly having love and passion in his life, trading it for friendship, companionship and for walking the path that he was expected to, she was also making that trade.

She did it with her eyes open. Because she had committed so hard to that life, to supporting him. Protecting him. Building a family with him.

She felt honor bound to continue doing it now.

But right now, she couldn't deny the ways that her feelings about Dionysus were different.

Utterly different.

It called to things inside of her that she had intentionally cut off. That she had intentionally decided to let go fallow.

Nuns married the church.

And she had married Theseus.

Both were an exercise in chastity and devotion.

Of course, Dionysus couldn't know that. Not now.

It would mean that she had failed at her mission. It was as simple as that.

Theseus's legacy was entirely in her hands now, and she would not falter. Otherwise what was the point of any of it? Of all these years.

He was gone, she didn't even have a child. If she lost control of the company...

Everything she had done... Starting with the moment that she had swerved away from Dionysus in the swimming hole, all of it, it would be *nothing*.

This was the last stretch. They'd been so close.

It wouldn't all fall because of her.

She could not face that. She could not turn around, look behind her and see nothing but ash. She was grieving. Grieving the loss of Theseus. Grieving the loss of her pregnancy. The loss of all that had come before, the work that she had put in, the sacrifices she had made would be too great to bear.

She simply could not.

"Come inside," he said, gesturing up the stairs.

She was grateful for the reprieve. Grateful for the break in the intensity of her thoughts. It was all too much. She could scarcely breathe past it.

So she focused on the tranquility and beauty of their surroundings. On the way the water dripped from the rocks, natural springs continuing their flow even around the house. Moss grew on the eaves. She saw the tree frog nestled in one of the deep-set windows.

"This is beautiful," she said.

"It reminded me very much of our swimming hole," he said.

It had been their swimming hole. Theseus hadn't particularly liked it. She and Dionysus had been the adventurous ones. The ones who were more independent.

Though Dionysus was far too independent. And she had taken her strength and used it to protect his brother.

She tried to let that make her angry. Except she couldn't, with any credibility allow that to infuriate her. Not when she knew that Theseus simply hadn't confided in Dionysus.

She could think of a thousand reasons why. The largest being that if Dionysus knew something like that, and their father decided to physically hurt him, then it would be a danger to Theseus, and Dionysus.

She knew that. So there was no point letting herself rewrite things and make it seem as if Dionysus couldn't be trusted. He had simply always and ever been another victim of their father.

Dionysus entered the code, which unlocked the door. The inside was much the same as the outside, in many ways. There were plants and stones, and a small river ran through the entry with a raised wooden platform going over the water.

"Why did you do this?"

"It was like that," he said. "I didn't want to disrupt the flow of the water."

This was his sanctuary. It suddenly made sense why he didn't invite people here. Why he didn't have parties here.

His life outside this place was loud. This was his touchstone with another time.

A time they had shared.

"It's beautiful."

"Thank you.

"All of the medical records from the spa facility have been sent to your doctor. She's on her way."

"Oh," she said. "Good. Great."

"If you don't feel ready yet…"

"I don't. But there are reasons…reasons we have to move quickly."

"Of course."

Still, she was stuck on the fact that somehow being pregnant with Dionysus's baby was different.

And with that came the discomforting thought that she might not be comfortable passing his baby off as Theseus's. Because he was right, what would she tell the child?

She pushed that to the side.

She walked into the beautiful dining area, where there was a long, natural wood table with raw edges beneath an entirely glass ceiling, windows allowing small shafts of light in, mostly shaded by the foliage all around.

There was a large platter of fruit sitting out waiting.

"Sit here," he said. "Have something to eat. When your doctor arrives, I'll let you know."

"Can I have some coffee?"

She hadn't been having caffeine, and now… She might as well.

"Of course," he said.

He disappeared, and she was left feeling… A strange sort of ache in her chest. When he returned a moment later with a mug of strong espresso, she looked up at him, their eyes clashing. She was very careful not to touch his fingers as she took the mug from his hand.

"Are you in the habit of making coffee for the women that stay with you?"

"No. Because women don't stay with me. If you're going to try to make this feel less heavy by diminishing me, you might as well stop. I can't remember the last time I made a cup of coffee for another person. I normally don't even make it for myself. Of course I know how. I'm not useless."

She stared at the coffee. At the small act of kindness. Yes, she was used to having drinks made for her. She and Theseus were incredibly wealthy, and she had been raised wealthy before that. But as a child whose parents had ignored her professionally she was keenly aware of the difference between someone being paid to complete a task that served you, and somebody in your life deciding to do something for you.

They were entirely different things.

And she was almost entirely unfamiliar with one of them.

When she took a sip of the coffee, she felt a strange emotion rising in her chest.

Before she could say another word to Dionysus, he was gone.

She sat there in the silence for a long moment, eating tropical fruit and drinking coffee. Her mind completely blank, because there were no words for what she had experienced in the past three weeks. None whatsoever.

It was all just tragedy.

It was all just… Crushing. But she was not crushed. She was still here.

Back on the island, and with Dionysus, which felt entirely symbolic of something she couldn't quite grasp hold of.

She sat like that until her doctor arrived an hour later, and Dionysus directed her and her physician to a bedroom upstairs.

It was plush and comfortable, though no amount of luxurious surroundings could make the examination, or the topic any easier.

"There's nothing physically wrong with you," she said. "Though, I would want to take precautions during labor and delivery, as I suspect you're prone to hemorrhage. But, likely there was simply something wrong with the development of the baby. These things do happen. The process of creating a human is quite complicated."

Ariadne nodded. "I know." She did. But it still felt something more than common when it was her. It still felt something more than the precariousness of life.

It felt personal. Like a dagger straight to her soul. But she imagined every woman in this position felt that way.

She wasn't a doctor. She was a woman who had lost the promise of a future that she had wanted desperately.

She could try again. She would try again. But it didn't

take the sting away from this moment. From this loss. The possibility of this child was gone forever, and she felt wounded by that.

"I would like you to wait at least one cycle. And then I come back for the insemination. He explained your situation to me."

She blinked. "He doesn't know. He doesn't know that this baby… The previous pregnancy, was conceived through insemination."

Her doctor looked at her, her gaze level. "And it isn't anyone's business but yours. You know that I am committed to keeping your confidence."

"Thank you. I will need you to keep confidence with this even more so."

"I understand. He did explain the situation."

"It is very important," said Ariadne, feeling like her doctor was judging her. Even though the other woman looked entirely nonjudgmental. But maybe Ariadne judged herself.

Maybe that was the problem.

She was the one who was worried that this decision was mercenary. She was the one that was worried it was heartless.

It was just she had to protect… Everyone. She just had to protect everyone.

The workers at the company, the memory of Theseus. Everyone.

"Four weeks… You're sure?"

"I would not feel comfortable performing the procedure prior to that. It's a little bit sooner than I would like. My preference would be to give you some normal cycles, but I understand that there is urgency here."

Of course, Ariadne knew that people got pregnant sooner than advised all the time. But she also understood that didn't involve doctors going against their medical inclinations.

That would require making a baby without medical intervention.

For a moment, the thought immobilized her. She was looking into Dionysus's eyes again in her memory.

No. She had to stop.

There would be no quicker way for Dionysus to find out the truth than for him to discover that his sister-in-law was still a virgin after spending eight years being married to his brother.

Even after being pregnant. Granted, she was reasonably certain the physical evidence of her virginity was long gone. But still, it would be obvious. She had no practical knowledge of how to touch a man.

Except for the once, she had only ever kissed a man as a performance. She and Theseus had kissed often. Their only truly passionate looking kiss being the one on their wedding day.

And after that, casual kisses to make them look like an affectionate couple. It had always made her feel warm. Happy in some ways. Connected. It didn't light her on fire.

It didn't feel like drinking a shot of whiskey.

She thought of Dionysus's eyes again.

And she pushed all of it to the side.

"I understand. I do. I want everything to be as safe as possible. I don't ever… I never want to go through something like that again."

"I know it's a lot," her doctor said. "I'm very sorry for everything you've been through." She put her hand on Ariadne's. And her first instinct was to pull away. Because this care, the softness, felt dangerous. It felt like an invitation to weakness, and Ariadne did not have the luxury of weakness.

After that, her doctor left and Ariadne opened up the closet, surprised to discover an entire wardrobe hanging there. Light-colored, floating linen things, that all looked incredibly friendly to spending time on an island.

She wasn't going to be able to try to conceive again for four weeks. There was really no point in her being here.

She had her computer, though, and she had conducted all of her meetings of late virtually. Why couldn't she do it here?

She could admit to herself, in this moment alone, that she might need to take this time to herself. That she might need to take this time to sit in some of these feelings. In grief.

She couldn't have her body being under undue stress when she was trying to prepare to conceive another baby.

Of course, there was no reason for Dionysus to stay,

and as she put on a navy-blue linen jumpsuit with wide legs that were both loose and flattering, she rehearsed what she was going to tell him in her mind.

She walked downstairs, expecting to find him sitting in the dining room, but he wasn't there.

She walked back into the far reaches of the house, and there was a low doorway that seemed to go into darkness.

Her breath left her body as she made her way through the craggy corridor, realizing that it was a cave. And then she saw light.

She walked into a massive chamber, well lit. The walls were limestone, almost white. And all around were beds of pink salt, and large glowing lamps made of the same material. The light it cast into the room was warm and rosy. But the biggest shock of all, was seeing Dionysus, sitting there in the middle of it all wearing nothing but a pair of white linen pants, his chest bare.

"What is this?"

"It's a cabin that I found here when I was a boy. I always wanted to build a house centered around a natural cave. I always felt as if there was a strong energy here. Or at least, it suited me to believe it. I used to come to this cave when I needed to heal from my father's latest beatings. Whether verbal or physical."

"Oh," she said.

She wasn't sure what to make of this. This insight into his mind. Into the fact that he believed in something… Almost metaphysical, even if he left space for the idea that it might be in his head. He had filled the place with pink sea salt, which she was sure she had read somewhere had some spiritual quality to it.

"I like it," he said. "Whether or not I believe it actually does me any good. It is a cathedral of sorts."

It was funny, how it reminded her of a large, stone cathedral in some ways.

"I can see that."

"And how was your appointment?"

"She wants me to wait until I have another period. I wanted to tell you, there is no reason for you to stay this whole time."

And then his eyes met hers, the light there immobilizing her. "I'm sorry, Ariadne. I'm afraid that you're stuck with me for the duration."

CHAPTER FIVE

SHE HAD BEEN lying low the past couple of weeks, slowly beginning to feel like her strength was coming back. Slowly shutting the symptoms of both her pregnancy and the pregnancy loss. The heaviness of everything was still there. But she felt… A sense of purpose, anyway.

She was thankful for James and his handling of things at Katrakis. Her phone call where she'd had to tell him about the miscarriage had been much harder.

I'm so sorry.

You don't have to be sorry, Ariadne.

But the baby mattered so much.

Not for the company. Not only the company. Because it had been part of Theseus.

Of course it did. But so do you.

I'm trying again but I know for you it won't be the same.

I still want to be involved.

Of course.

James was one of her best friends. How could she not love him when meeting him had changed everything for Theseus? After a lifetime of isolation James had truly brought him to life.

It was the one comfort she had. That Theseus had been in love when he'd died. That he'd had that joy. That he'd had hope.

But they should have been able to have a life together.

That had been the plan.

She thought of Theseus's ashes, safely kept at their home, because right now choosing a resting place for them felt wrong when…when what would be written on the stone would have to be a lie.

When James couldn't be mentioned.

James and Theseus had met and fallen in love when James had taken a CFO position at Katrakis—as it had become clear neither Theseus nor Ariadne were a fit for the role. The connection had been instant.

Ariadne had encouraged it. She'd never seen Theseus so happy.

He'd been with James for three years when he'd told Ariadne he couldn't keep his sexuality a secret for the rest of his life.

Lavender marriages are so Victorian, Ari.

As are we, Theseus.

What if we weren't? What if after we have a baby, after the inheritance is set, we divorce. And I… I could marry James and you could marry whoever you like.

That had been the plan. And when they'd started trying to have a baby the plan had also included James coparenting that child. It was why he shared in the loss too.

Everything wasn't lost. She refused to let herself feel like it was.

Because she and Dionysus would find their way through this. They would... They would have a baby.

Well, she would.

She needed to get out of the house. She had been babying herself indoors, only venturing out to the patio at the side of her room, which was a lovely grotto with rock walls all around it, and vines growing down the sides of them.

There was a little table and chairs there, and she felt secluded within the walls.

But she felt... A restless spirit beginning to rise up inside of her. Because she had been free here once. She had been a child, filled with hope and joy.

She had found a sort of joy in her life in the time since.

But she had never been as happy as she was here. The summers that she had spent roaming around with Dionysus had been the happiest. And yet...

She had given him up.

She pushed her guilt aside.

He had never made any declarations toward her. They had been friends. He had kissed her, and she still didn't know...

He wants what I have.

Theseus had said that, angry after Dionysus had kissed her.

She wondered if that was true. Dionysus had never acted jealous of Theseus, not in her presence, but maybe he was. He was the younger brother, after all. He wasn't going to inherit anything. He had had to make it on his own, and maybe that had caused more strife between them than she had realized.

He made light of it, even now. Using it as a trinket to hold up in front of her, to bait her. Goad her. If it had mattered to him at all he wouldn't have done that.

She felt like he'd done it…she had never understood why.

She was his friend, she always had been. And there had been moments of tension between them. But if he'd had feelings for her…he'd certainly never said. Dionysus seemed like a man who would say.

She'd wondered if it was a joke. She'd always been secretly afraid it might be. Though, she didn't know if the alternative was better.

She rummaged through the clothes and found a bathing suit. It was shockingly brief, bright orange with triangle shaped cups that had a ruffled edge. The bottoms barely covered her bottom, and she squinted at herself in the mirror. She looked… Disturbingly good. She didn't like clothes that were overly sexy, because it… It implied a desire to attract attention. And she was never comfortable using her body in that way. She liked to look nice, of course. What woman didn't?

But she tried to look classy. Not…

She was alone on an island. Well. Mostly alone. A disquieting feeling went through her, and she felt a strange sensation between her thighs.

She wasn't really alone.

She sucked her breath in through her teeth and then grabbed a white dress and put it over the top of the bikini.

It suited her skin tone, and made her eyes look even brighter green.

When she slipped outside, the air was sultry, and it made her feel… Younger. Like she belonged here.

Like a wood nymph.

As she began to walk down a path that led to where, she didn't know, she felt some of her burdens rolling off of her shoulders. She let herself forget.

Who she was. What had happened to her. She let herself forget all of her pain. Everything.

She looked at the trees, at the flowers.

And she remembered. Everything had been so beautiful here. They hadn't been carefree. No. They had been something even more poignant. More intense. They knew how difficult life could be. And they had appreciated the glory of having this place. Having friends.

That almost made her want to weep, because it was such a simple sentiment.

And yet so real. So true.

She kept on walking until sweat beaded on the back of her neck, and she was beginning to wish that she had some respite from the heat. And that was when she heard running water.

It was the waterfall. She knew it. She was thrilled that she had somehow directed herself toward that familiar place, even though it had been so long since she was here. Even though she was disoriented by the change in landmarks.

She paused for a moment and tried to orient herself. The waterfall was in front of her somewhere, which meant that her parents' house was behind her when it had stood.

But somewhere past where Dionysus had built his home.

From there, she could figure out the direction of the beach. The direction of some of their favorite caves.

A thrill went through her. She began to move more quickly, that feeling of being unencumbered moving with her.

She moved nimbly over the rocky path, and when she came to the waterfall she stripped her dress off without thinking about it. And she dove straight into the clear blue pool.

The water was cool and clear. Perfect.

This had been their place. Their blue lagoon. Where she and Dionysus had gone to get completely away from the adults. They had talked about their hopes and dreams. They had talked about what a monster his father was, and what a useless fool hers was. He had talked about his car.

It made her smile.

He had kept the car. He had bought the island.

He was an extraordinarily sentimental person for all that he pretended not to be. For all that he pretended that no one and nothing meant much of anything to him.

But then… Who had he had in his life?

He was right, he and Theseus had been distant. She didn't think that Theseus had held onto his anger over the kiss, but perhaps he had.

At the very least, he had been afraid to be too close to his brother. For fear that Dionysus would realize that the marriage wasn't everything that it seemed.

But it was so difficult to get him to open up on that topic.

She submerged underneath the water, and she let those thoughts float away. She let herself think of nothing but the moment. But the cool of the water, the sound of the waterfall. She treaded water, kicking her feet to keep herself afloat.

And then she heard a splash come from behind her.

She turned, just in time to see Dionysus surface above the water.

"How did you know I was here?" she asked.

He grinned, and her heart clenched painfully.

It was… It really was like being in the past. And she wanted to cling to that. She wanted to leave all of the baggage, all of the pain, somewhere else.

"This is where you always are," he said.

Her heart lifted.

"It's my favorite place on the island."

"Completely unspoiled," he said.

"A good thing neither of our fathers ever explored beyond the confines of their very comfortable houses. Or they might have figured out that they could monetize it, and then it never would've stayed unspoiled."

"True," he said.

"I finally felt like getting out," she said.

"Good," he said.

The sun reflected off the water, casting a glow on his face. It made him look younger. More carefree. It added to the illusion.

"Tell me about your business. Why did you decide to do... Delivery."

"I thought it was amusing. Because I thought that it was rather like shipping. But on a smaller, more personal scale. It turned out that people were ready for the convenience. It has been good for me."

"Poking at your father even while you separated yourself entirely?"

"I wouldn't be me if I didn't."

"No. I guess you wouldn't."

"My father was very hard on Theseus." His expression went remote. "He demanded absolute perfection from him. In a way he didn't for me. But if I acted up enough, I could draw fire. And if I can keep him distracted, then he left Theseus alone."

"Poor Theseus," she said, her chest clenching. "It was always hard for him."

"Yes," said Dionysus, though his voice went hard.

She swam nearer to Dionysus, but he moved away. And she couldn't help but feel as if she had missed something. As if… She had done something wrong. But she didn't want to ask. She wanted to bask in good feelings. And nostalgia. She didn't want to turn over rocks or dredge up skeletons.

They had had a rather unhappy childhood. Except for this.

"Remember when you told me that fairies lived here. And that the water was enchanted."

"Did I tell you that?"

She studied him closely. "Yes. I don't believe that you forgot it either. Because I don't believe you forget anything."

"That is possible," he said.

"More than possible."

"All right. I do remember that I made up a story. But to be fair, I heard a bit of it from the cook. It was a legend about this island. That it was enchanted. That's why it's so lush. Even though it can get dry here. It is different. Unlike any place else."

"It is," she said. "I know I was never as happy when we were in the States. In New York I felt so lonely, even surrounded by thousands of people on every street. Here, I was often alone, and yet I never really felt by myself."

"It's the land. I feel connected to it too. I always have."

"What was it like? When you weren't here?"

"Surely Theseus must've told you."

"He told me what it was like for him. What was it like for you?"

"My father was exacting and cruel at times. He took pleasure in setting tasks he knew were relatively impossible so that he could punish us. He said that was how life was. That good enough didn't exist. And you must always strive, even knowing that there will always be a punishment waiting."

"What did he do to you."

"He particularly liked to isolate me. He tried fists, but at a certain point I hit him back." His expression went hollow. "He realized that threatening Theseus had a far greater effect on me than that. That was why I never did it again. It wasn't worth it. Because he would see Theseus punished, and I could not... I couldn't stand that. What he began to do instead was separating us. Isolating us. He made me worry for him. I don't know what he told Theseus about me."

"He told Theseus that you were away. Partying."

His face went sharp. "What?"

"That's what Theseus said. He... He was angry about that. He felt like you left and got a reprieve, and that your father was hardest on him."

"That bastard. No. I spent that time locked away in an attic. Until I figured out how to scale down the house, but even then, I wasn't off pleasing myself. I would just go back into the woods behind the house."

"Oh, Dionysus…"

"Don't," he said. "No wonder my brother thought the worst of me."

"He didn't. Yes, he had some issues. But… He loved you."

She moved closer to him, and suddenly realized her mistake. Because he was looking at her, intent in his dark eyes.

"Do you remember when it was just us?" And she didn't know if he meant that first few moments of the conversation they were just having, or if she meant the time in the pool when he had captured her in his arms. She could remember how strong his body was. She had been laughing. He swam to her then, and she realized why he had moved away before. Because there was something powerful throbbing between them, and it was unwelcome.

But she didn't move. She stayed there like that, entranced.

"Here we find ourselves," he said, his voice filled with wonder.

"Dionysus…"

But everything, all her words, her intent, died on her lips just then.

He moved to her, and then he reached out and touched her face, moved the water droplet away from her cheek, his thumb over her lips.

"Ariadne. Don't you know if there was anything enchanted here, it was always you. Just you."

For the moment, everything stood still. There was nothing but this. Nothing but him and her. And the silence between them.

"I wasn't the only one who thought so."

His voice was rough. He moved away from her abruptly and she felt…bereft.

She knew why he wouldn't close the distance between them. And she should be grateful.

Instead she felt a kernel of something close to anger building in her chest.

Theseus wasn't here anymore. Yet she still felt…tied to him. To his legacy. To what they'd built together. How could she abandon it all now?

How could she undermine it all with Dionysus.

It was her turn to jolt.

She swam toward the bank and climbed out of the water, moving toward her clothes. She'd lost herself for a moment. She'd lost her focus.

She had let herself go too far back in time.

She'd lost herself.

She had to remember what mattered.

Theseus's legacy.

When she got back to her room she felt cold.

"Theseus is dead." She said it out loud.

Theseus was dead and she was still here. And in spite of herself, the anger she'd felt when Dionysus moved away from her continued to burn.

CHAPTER SIX

IT WASN'T HIS plan to be here with his sister-in-law for that length of time. But now that he had made his decision, he would not correct course.

Three weeks since he had come to the island with her, and the week of potential conception was closer than he'd like.

He sneered even standing in the room alone. *Conception.* With medical instruments. Things like this tempted him to believe in God. Because it seemed as if whoever ran the cosmos had quite a lot of intent.

Making a baby with her this way, passing the child off as his brother's…

He couldn't help but think Theseus was demanding his pound of flesh from beyond the grave.

In this, he and his twin were alike.

He was not a man who did things by half measures. And he was determined to make sure that Ariadne was well cared for.

The glittering, refined relationship that Ariadne and Theseus presented to the public might have been mysterious to him, but the truth was, Ariadne had always seemed well cared for by Theseus.

One thing he knew for certain, was that Theseus would see Ariadne cared for. Because of that, Dionysus would see it done as well.

But being around her was… Its own sort of challenge.

He brought in some household staff to help make sure that she was cared for adequately. To ensure that she had all of the food and necessary blankets and anything else that she might require.

For his part, he spent much of his time in his office, working. Followed by periods of strenuous outdoor activity. Including rock-climbing, swimming laps in the sea, and any other method he could think to thoroughly exhaust himself.

He hadn't been lying when he'd told her that he often felt peace when he was in the cave in the house.

There was something about this place. Something about the nature here. Or perhaps, it was simpler than that.

For him, there had never been a happier time than when they had spent summers on this island.

It had been the only time they'd had freedom. He wondered if that was why it had been difficult for Theseus. Perhaps it wasn't happy for his brother to have moments where he felt like their childhood might be normal. It didn't bother Dionysus to take a vacation from the unending iron fist of their father.

Yes, it was always waiting back home for them.

But the afternoons...

They belonged to the rocks and the trees. They belonged to the water.

He could never be sorry for those moments of peace. Of sanity.

Though, he had to admit now that perhaps some of it was the feel of her, saturating the place. Covering each memory in a sort of golden sunshine that had never been quite the same without her.

But she was here now.

The tension it created inside of him was unexpected.

Because he had been certain he had left behind any unwanted feelings for her the night of her birthday party.

Any that had lingered, were dealt with swiftly and brutally when they popped up. He had rearranged himself entirely after that.

And yet this prolonged exposure to her...

Typically, he left her to her own devices. Typically, he had his staff care for her. But he had woken up this morning aware of the fact that it was her birthday. Her birthday, in the middle of all of this loss. And whatever conflict he felt, he was not conflicted over the fact that she deserved some sort of acknowledgment.

After all, at one time, she had been one of his only friends.

His brother was the other.

There were not two people in the world he had cared for more. Theirs had been a bond he hadn't quite understood, and he'd felt on the outside of it. He was a blunt instrument. A fighter. And while he'd wanted to find his way into that relationship, to be closer to both of them, he hadn't fully known how.

He hadn't known how to do it without breaking something.

Now Theseus wasn't here.

But Ariadne was.

He tasked the kitchen with making her favorite cake. He remembered well from their teenage years. Her eighteenth birthday.

He had made her cake. He had intended to give it to her.

We're engaged.

He threw the cake in the trash. She never knew about it.

Instead he'd kissed her. And his brother had taken hold of him with iron in his grip. Ariadne had looked shocked.

Still, now that meant he knew exactly what she liked. He made sure to have his staff create something suitably rich for her. He made sure that there was a spread of her favorite, freshly made pastas, and salads. Along with fresh baked bread.

Perhaps an attempt to prove to himself that he'd changed. That he could acknowledge this without thinking of the kiss.

He'd had so many women since then.

That the memory of her mouth continued to haunt him seemed improbable.

A reminder, he was certain now, of all the ways he'd managed to fail in the protection of his brother. Perhaps if that had never happened, Theseus wouldn't have frozen him out. Maybe he would have called Dionysus and told him how much he was struggling.

There isn't anything to be done about it now.

When Ariadne came downstairs, wrapped in bright pink silk, he questioned his own sanity in this farcical re-creation of a time best forgotten.

She looked better than she had only a week ago. Stronger. A little bit less haunted.

"Oh," she said. "I didn't expect to see you here."

"It is your birthday," he said.

Her eyes flared. "You remembered."

It struck him as a very odd thing to say. Remembering implied that it was something he had to think of. Something he didn't simply know. And the truth was, he knew her birthday. Just as he knew his own. He felt it coming on like a change in the weather. A whisper across the wind reminding him that it was close to the time when Ariadne had first come into the world.

How could he forget, when he'd exposed his own heart so badly on her eighteenth birthday.

He'd changed since then. The lessons his father had taught him hadn't taken hold yet when he was a young man, but that moment with Ariadne had been clear.

Maybe he was insane. It had been suggested a time or

two. That in his mad pursuit of wealth, and his dogged pursuit of pleasure, he had lost some piece of himself. Or some piece of civility, anyway.

Except…

He had never wanted to be his father anyway.

And while his brother had certainly taken an admirable path in life, that wasn't him either.

Maybe in order to succeed the way that he had a bit of insanity was required.

And if that meant time in the wilderness, and the feeling of Ariadne's birthday as if it was an oncoming season, then so be it.

"Yes," he said simply. And nothing at all about seasons.

"You… You decided to have dinner with me for my birthday."

"When we were on the island, I never missed it."

"Of course not. But we were all here together."

"As we are now."

He extended a hand, and only when she took it, her silken skin sliding against his, did he realize that it might've been a mistake.

Because touching her…

He had a vivid flashback then. Of a time when they had been younger. When they had very nearly…

Or perhaps she hadn't. But he certainly had.

Maybe a kiss hadn't been on her mind that moment they had made eye contact in the water. Maybe she hadn't been thinking what it would feel like for their mouths to touch. For their slick, wet skin to glide together. Maybe she hadn't wondered what it would be like if they lost their senses and claimed each other completely beneath the warmth of the sun.

But he had.

He had been a virgin then. Because of her.

He had lost his head at her eighteenth birthday, because of her and she'd been certain that he'd done it to hurt her. Trick her. Like they hadn't been friends before.

He'd had plenty of opportunity to be with someone. But he hadn't wanted anyone else. It was only when Theseus had made his announcement that Dionysus…

Of course after the engagement announcement, and after the kiss, he'd realized what a fool he was.

Ariadne had not been waiting for him.

And if in that water Ariadne had felt an attraction toward him, if she had responded to his kiss, it had likely been because he looked exactly like his brother. Because his brother was who she wanted.

He could see how the attraction between them had been a confusing thing for her. It had sure as hell confused him as a teenage boy longing for any touch, any hint she wanted him. But it was Theseus she'd loved.

He just happened to look like him.

And he would do well to remember that.

Still, it didn't change the fact that through all the years, in spite of all the other women, in spite of her marriage to his brother, the fact that she had been pregnant with his child, he wanted her.

Perhaps she remained unfinished business. For he was not foolish enough to believe in love. Not now.

He had left that childish dream behind long ago. In that sense, he was thankful. And Theseus and Ariadne had married each other.

It was Theseus who had broken her heart. Theseus who had failed her.

Had Dionysus married her, right now, he would have been the one to fail.

His father was a monster. And he was not that manner of monster. But his father had broken something in him.

When he had told her he didn't wish to be a father, he had spoken the truth.

He did not wish to impose himself upon a child.

He would not even know where to begin.

It would be as foolish as taking a wife.

Foolishness at the highest level.

But today was her birthday. And he would honor that. Because while there was no scope for forever in him, between them, or between himself or anyone else, there was this moment.

The space of time where he was dedicated to…

Martyrdom?

What a strange pursuit for a libertine.

Though, if he were honest, his self-indulgence was a form of self-denial.

He had more sex than most. More partners than he could count.

And yet, never the one that he had wanted first.

Never the one he had wanted most.

He had not anticipated having a revelation standing there before Ariadne, and that dress that clung to her curves.

Dionysus was a martyr.

Here he was, sharing a home with his brother's wife, who he wanted more than he could recall ever wanting another thing. His one experience of self-denial, and he savored and cherished that self-denial. Held it close to his heart. It was why he could never quite let go of Ariadne. And now he was considering giving her a child which she would pass off as Theseus's. Completing the metaphor, in many ways. Because he felt that she should have always been his first. And yet she had given herself to his brother. A body that had felt innately his from the moment he had begun to recognize her as a woman.

Was that perhaps why he could not let her go?

Did he get something out of that core of self-denial?

Perhaps he just didn't know how to let go of the pain he had been raised on.

"I had the chef prepare a selection of your favorites," he said, gesturing toward the dining room. The table was laden with food. All of her very favorite things, cheeses and meats, kebabs and flatbread with dips.

And that chocolate cake, marvelous, at the far end of the table.

Her eyes went round. "This is far too much."

"It is just enough, to celebrate your birthday. Given everything."

"Is this a pity banquet?" Her delicate brows knit together, but there was a small glint of humor in her eyes, and that reminded him of bygone days.

"Obviously. Nothing more than pity chocolate cake."

"Well, since you've gone to so much trouble. Or rather, your chef has."

She stepped inside, and he noted the tears sparkling in her eyes.

"Don't cry," he said.

She looked over at him. "All I've done is cry. For weeks now."

His chest went tight. He hated to see her sad.

"Well. Stop. I'm trying to give you something nice."

"It is the niceness that makes me cry. Because I don't think I have been on the receiving end of your kindness in years."

"Have I not been kind?"

"Things have not been like they were."

"We shared many meals together in the past several years."

"It isn't the same. We were real friends once."

She wouldn't allow him to trip her up or play games of any kind. It was one of the things he admired about her. But also one of the things that he found singularly irritating.

Because he did know. There was a wall between

himself and Ariadne, and had been ever since she had married Theseus. Just as there had been a wall between himself and Theseus.

"I loved my brother," he said. "And I do not wish to turn your birthday dinner into a eulogy. So I will say this once, and then we will be done with the topic. I loved my brother, but I did not know how to relate to him. The way that he chose to deal with my father was entirely opposed to my own method. I don't blame him. I do not think what he did was wrong. Except that it made him miserable. It was not you, Ariadne. That we can be certain."

"It wasn't only your father either. Theseus made choices about how he wanted to live his life. He made choices about how he wanted to be seen by the public. There were… Pressures that your father put on him, yes. But he took them to heart. And no matter how much I tried… He was rigid in that. He refused to change his perspective."

"So you see, there was a wall there, you are correct. Because I wanted to tell him he did not have to be our father's puppet. And I wanted to tell you that you didn't have to be that perfect accessory to that life."

"It was complicated by the fact that your father demanded a level of compliance in order for Theseus to maintain control of the company."

"I understand that. As did you. But it didn't stop you from wishing he would change things, did it?"

She shook her head. "No. I would have had him be happier."

"Yes," he said. "Of course you would."

He looked at her, and he wondered why she thought he hadn't been *happy*. He'd had no call to not be. Theseus had Ariadne.

And weren't you just thinking only a moment ago that if you'd had Ariadne you would have found a way to ruin it?

Dionysus had a feeling his own failure would have been to burn them both out. To ruin what might have been beautiful if he were not...

Himself.

"But now that has to shift. The focus is on you," he said.

"The focus *has* been on me. Entirely, for these past weeks. Ever since... Ever since the funeral. And then the miscarriage, and now I'm here. Everything has been about me."

"No. Everything has been about the tragedy. You're sure you want to have a child? You can do whatever you wanted. You are not bound to Theseus anymore."

It seemed as if it had never occurred to her. Something like wistfulness passed over her face, and a deeper, more complex emotion that rocked him down to his soul.

Made him feel adrift. And he didn't do adrift. He filled that restless void. With drink. With sex. Overindulgence.

And here he was sitting at a banquet, and yet in the land of self-denial.

Because what he truly wanted, he could not have.

What he truly wanted, he would destroy.

"I committed myself to him," she said.

"I would like to have a conversation with you that has nothing to do with him." It wasn't fair. It bordered on cruel. But he hated that even after he'd died, his brother still stood between them.

"I don't know that it's possible," she said. "Not now. Although... It may be hard to understand, but I really do believe in what he was doing. It matters to me. I like the work that I do."

"And running the company, that is your dream?"

"Yes."

"And a baby?"

She nodded slowly. "My parents have never had anything to do with me. My mother went back to modeling and traveling when she divorced my father and I never lived with her. My father was always more interested in his newest lover. If I am ever going to have a family. If I am ever going to have that connection, it will have to come from me."

"And if you meet another man? And fall in love?"

"I will never forget my marriage to your brother. He will always be one of the most important people who has ever been in my life. I won't wish it away, any more than I would wish away a child that represented that union."

"But you'll know the child isn't his," he said, unable to stop himself from poking.

"I know a lot of things," she said.

But she didn't elaborate. Instead she began to fill her plate with food, and he realized that they had no small talk between them. They had simply known one another for too long. And yet there was distance there. Distance could not be bridged by talking about favorite movies and the weather. And they would both know that it was a counterfeit attempt at filling the silence if they attempted it. So instead he reached into memory. One that had nothing to do with Theseus.

"Do you remember when we stole champagne from your father's party."

Her eyes lit up and for a moment he felt like he'd conquered the world. For a moment, Ariadne didn't look sad. "And strawberry cake."

What a rare thing to share a memory with her that didn't have teeth.

"Yes. We hid out in the back in the darkness and overindulged."

She laughed. "I had forgotten about that. We were... Perhaps fifteen and seventeen?"

"Something like that," he said. He shook his head. "Theseus was of course far too strict with himself to engage in such activities."

She laughed. "It would never have occurred to him."

"But it did occur to us."

"Yes," she said. "It did."

"We were incorrigible at times."

"But our parents were terrible all the time. And we were always trying to figure out how to make some joy out of what we were given. That was my favorite thing about you," she said. "You taught me how to have fun. Otherwise, I was just alone in my father's house, rattling around, feeling isolated. But you showed me that I could make fun out of anything. More and less responsibly, depending on the moment in time, I grant you. But... The most important thing was that we laughed. We created things to smile about, even when there was nothing."

He had never once seen himself that way. He'd done his best to protect Theseus. He'd misbehaved as a matter of distraction. That was all. He'd seen himself as something dark and unwieldy not...

Not as a source of joy for her.

Of happiness.

It rocked him for a moment. He wouldn't let it be two.

"That is why I love this place," he said, as close as he could ever get to revealing his own deep wounds. "Because for me it is not the site of pain. But of joy. Of the ways that we found to make a bit of happiness. Before we went off into the real world."

"Do you find joy out there?" she asked. "You took a very different path than I did."

She didn't mention Theseus. But then, he wondered if she looked at him and saw herself. Because they had been alike then.

"I have decided that the concept of finding joy is far too nebulous. I have decided instead to embrace all forms of momentary, fleeting pleasure that I can find, because happiness is temporary, and false besides. You think that I'm different. That I've changed. The truth is, I think it does harden you to live as I have. But I never possessed the ability to be self-contained. And now that I've changed in this way, now that I have decided to seek my own pleasure, to put my own desires above anything else, I have found a lot more joy in isolation. A birthday party for one, if you will."

"But you don't understand," she said, her face suddenly grave. "That Theseus never had that option."

"There is always an option, Ariadne. Always. I chose the life I live. But Theseus chose his."

"It wasn't so simple for him. Your father built a cage around him when he was a child. He spent his life fighting. To have what he deserved in spite of your father, and to try and make joy where he could."

"You make it sound like it was such a battle for him," he said, the words acidic. "He had the company. He had our father's approval. He had *you*. He had a baby on the way. He had everything."

"He didn't," she said, her voice clipped. "He…he lived in fear most of his life. It was only in the past few years… Dionysus." She looked up at him, tears sliding down her cheek. "Did you really never guess?"

"What?"

There was something in her eyes, something haunted

and hopeless, something that tore at his gut and made him question everything. Her. Himself.

And most of all Theseus.

"Theseus and I had a marriage in name only, Dionysus. I swore to him that I would marry him. I promised. When I was fifteen I promised him, because I held him as he told me he could never be what your father needed him to be. Because he was gay, Dionysus. And he spent his whole life trying to make it go away, trying to hide it. Until he fell in love. And then he decided he was going to *live*. He meant to live. For his child, but most of all for himself. He was finally going to be true to himself and now he's gone, and he never can be. He didn't have it all. He spent his life living a lie and not even you ever guessed the truth."

CHAPTER SEVEN

SHE PRAYED FOR FORGIVENESS. Wherever Theseus was, she could only pray that he could forgive her. And she prayed for forgiveness from her own self, because even as the words hung there in the air between them, her lips cold, she felt anger at her own weakness.

She hoped James would forgive her. For saying this now when it was never out in the open while Theseus was with him.

She felt like a failure for saying it out loud when Theseus hadn't been able to.

For telling Dionysus when she knew full well Theseus had hoped to tell his brother himself one day.

But she couldn't stand it anymore. She couldn't stand walking on eggshells. She couldn't stand making the wrong apologies for her husband. For herself. She couldn't stand his idea that Theseus had an easy, perfect life without pain, when she knew that he had suffered.

And in that moment, one thing was clear enough. Theseus's pain deserved to be acknowledged. Not erased.

So did his love. The love he'd shown her as a friend.

The love he'd found with James. A testament to his resilience and strength and to the enduring power of hope that could live inside a person.

Theseus wasn't his suffering. He was more than that. But she also couldn't stand Dionysus writing his life off as easy.

He had no idea.

"That is *impossible*," he said, his expression one of utter shock.

"It isn't only *possible*, it's *true*."

He said nothing for a long moment. "You've known, all this time?"

She exhaled slowly. "I was his wife. Of course I knew."

"For how long?"

"Always," she said softly.

He shook his head. "How?"

"He told me," she whispered. "When we were teenagers. You have no idea... He was so ashamed of it. He wasn't... You. He wanted to be you, Dionysus. You were more what your father wanted."

It was Dionysus's turn to laugh, though it was humorless. "I was not what my father wanted. I never have been. My father hated us both. Perhaps for different reasons, but... I will always believe what he hated was that he could not inject himself into us and live life over again. What he hates is his own mortality. Watching us walk around, young, with our lives ahead, and his mostly behind him. And so he set out to try and mold us exactly how he wanted. I refused. But it had the side effect of drawing fire away from Theseus."

"Theseus saw you as the masculine ideal. He wanted to be like you. Everything would've been easier for him if he could have been. He was quieter, and he was… He lived so much inside of himself, and I don't know if that was because of his secret, or if it was because it was simply who he was. It took a toll on him. Of course it did. He didn't want to live in secret, he wanted to be like anyone else. He wanted a partner and a family. And I know that I don't have to explain to you why he had to keep it a secret."

"Why did he keep it a secret from me?" Dionysus asked, his eyes blazing.

"He…"

"He didn't trust me," said Dionysus.

She was silent for a moment. "Do you blame him?"

"Because of your birthday party," he asked.

"Yes."

"If he wasn't in love with you, why was it such a betrayal?"

She looked at him, his dark eyes piercing her. And it forced her memory back.

She remembered Dionysus sweeping across the expanse and taking her in his arms. She hadn't thought. She couldn't remember actually applying a name to that lean, hungry face. The expression in his eyes nothing like Theseus's. They weren't identical. They never had been.

It was only after Theseus had come out and seen them. And she had… She had panicked. She had pushed him away. She'd sworn to Theseus she'd been disoriented and had been convinced it was him.

She had wanted so badly to forget it, to forget the way that it had lit her skin on fire. Her first kiss. Her first kiss had been from her brother-in-law, and it had been the passion she had dreamed of finding with Theseus. It had been confusing. And she had been trapped anyway.

"You knew we were together. That we intended to marry and you kissed me anyway. I was his life raft."

"What a flattering designation."

She ignored that. "It was more complicated than that …we were best friends. He was like a brother to me in so many ways."

"I actually was his brother. His twin."

"Yes. And he didn't want you to…see him as less."

"I wouldn't have," Dionysus said.

"I know. I do know that but you have to understand he hated himself so much, for so many years, and I was the only person he trusted. In many ways we were more than friends because for years I was the only one who really got to know him. I was the only one he let know him." She paused. "It changed. He met someone and it changed. He started to be himself with a growing group of people."

"Still not me."

"He needed it to be…a new life. A new thing. It was too hard for him to try and revisit old wounds."

"Why was I a wound?"

"Because he associated you too much with your father. With his own...failures, I think. But isn't that the real tragedy of your father? He chose Theseus as his favored son, which put him under a pressure he could never live up to and you, you who would have been much more able to be the alpha heir he wanted, were his chosen second."

"Are you saying I'm more like my father?"

She shook her head. "No. But he would see himself more in you. What man wouldn't? Adventurous. Successful with women."

"So flattering, Ariadne."

"I'm not trying to flatter you. I'm trying to make you see. Your father styled you both as players in a game neither of you could win, partly because of the roles he cast you in. It was easier for Theseus when he was removed from the game. When we had the power to make Katrakis what we saw it could be. When he met James. Who is just...the most wonderful man, he truly is. He helped Theseus find himself." She blinked back tears. "I'll love him for that forever."

Dionysus looked pained, but it passed quickly. "And where is James now?"

"He's the CFO of Katrakis, he's covering for me in my absence and in general keeping all of my secrets, still. I had to tell him about the baby. He..." She blinked.

"He wanted the child too."

She nodded, grateful that at least Dionysus could

understand that. "Theseus and I were going to divorce. Once all of the inheritance was set in stone for us and our baby we were going to divorce and he was going to marry James. With my blessing."

"You didn't love him?"

"I did. Desperately. I will mourn Theseus for the rest of my life. But I didn't love him as a wife. He was a kind of soulmate, but it wasn't a romance. Not ever."

"The child…"

"I was artificially inseminated. I never slept with your brother."

There were so many bombs now laying on the table between them. So many twisted, tangled truths.

Because if you pulled that one thread in the tapestry it threatened to unravel them all.

It frightened her, because these were all things she had never voiced before.

"You have to walk me through everything. From the beginning. From the day that he told you, to your eighteenth birthday." He let out a hard breath. "To now."

"Okay," she said, nodding slowly. "I always felt protective of him. It felt like falling in love. I wanted to keep him safe. You and I could run across the island together, we were fools together. Theseus…"

"He was more reserved," he said.

"Yes. But then I discovered that it was more than that. He wasn't just reserved. He was frightened. He was angry."

"He never seemed angry."

"He was. At himself. For so many years, Dionysus."

"Why didn't you tell me? When you asked to have a baby with me?"

"An element of it is the inheritance, I won't lie. Because of course your father could still take that away."

"And you don't trust me either."

"No. That isn't it. I just think the less said out loud the better. But also…it is his story. And I wanted to honor that this story, his story, was very personal and painful for him. And then he found James, and that means there is another person involved who is still very much alive. Who is…grieving and who loved him and who can't acknowledge that love right now and when the truth comes out—because he wanted it to—James has to be part of that decision."

She couldn't read his face. She wished, not for the first time, that they'd stayed as close as they had when they were younger. But it had been impossible. She was keeping secrets—some Theseus's and some her own.

She wanted to comfort him. She wanted, right then, for things to be different, but the distance between them hadn't been down to Theseus entirely. It had been her.

The memory of the kiss, and the knowing the kiss had brought.

Because after that she could never pretend to be ignorant of why she felt a pull toward him that was so very different than the one she felt for Theseus.

She had wanted to get rid of the imprint of his lips on hers, the heat of it all.

When she thought of it, she did her best only ever to think of her upset. How angry she had been.

How betrayed.

Because thinking about anything else was… Even now, as he looked at her, her skin burned.

And it wasn't shame that she felt.

Regrettably.

How could she? Talking about Theseus's pain at the same time she was looking at Dionysus and remembering what it had been like when he had claimed her mouth with his?

How dare she, when she had just lost Theseus's baby?

Maybe she was like her father after all. Perhaps she would have found it easy to find new lovers and then discard them.

Except, you never touched Theseus. And Dionysus has always been a problem.

Even worse. She would be the discarded.

Because she knew how that kind of thing works. One thing that he had said to her when they had sat down to dinner stuck with her. Her life did not have to be about Theseus anymore.

She needed space. Time. That didn't mean she wasn't ready to make the decision about the baby, she knew that was the right thing to do. But thinking about anything physical with anyone, let alone Dionysus was… Absolutely not.

She had been bound by vows since she was fifteen years old.

The last thing she would ever do is jump into something so complicated. As if having a baby with him, no matter the method wouldn't be complicated.

She had told herself that it could be the same, but when had Dionysus and Theseus ever been the same?

She had told herself she could ignore Dionysus, but when had she ever been able to do that?

For one fleeting moment she imagined running away. Leaving behind the company. Leaving behind everything. And for a moment, it felt freeing. For a moment, it felt exhilarating. But then she imagined herself, alone, falling through space.

With nothing and nobody. Without the found family she had made at the shipping company. Without any lingering connection even to Dionysus.

She couldn't bear it.

She couldn't bear it.

"Even if you can't understand," she said, reinforcing all of it within herself as much as she was doing anything else, "it's what I have worked for. I care about Katrakis Shipping. I have put my heart and soul into it. As much as I put my heart and soul into trying to make Theseus happy. Again, you might not understand. But he was my best friend. We might not have been in love, not romantically, but I did love him. Were your parents happy?"

"Of course not," the Dionysus. "Nobody could ever have been happy with my father."

"And you know all about my parents. My father

traded in wives like they were cars. Every couple of years he wanted a new model with better features.

"That is my expectation of romance. That it's fleeting. At best. The friendship that I had with Theseus, that wasn't fleeting. It was real. A real commitment to being a family."

"And that's all you think you want?"

"That's all I really want to invest in. Even if you can't understand it, you must… You must be able to get it. I want to build something that lasts. Something where…"

"Where people need you?"

His words might as well have been a blade.

"What's wrong with that? At least people can depend on me. You're out there alone, caring for nothing and no one."

"I also run a company that benefits thousands of employees worldwide, do you not think in that sense I take care of people in the same way you do?"

"It's different."

"Why? You fancy that it's different because you know their names? Because you have taken something that was bad and made it better? I am not denigrating the achievement, but it seems rather hypocritical that it matters when you do it, but doesn't matter when I do."

"It's only that… I gave you the opportunity to tell me about your life. You make it sound like you don't have any connections."

"I don't. You're correct about that. But I suppose my conclusion has been the opposite to yours. There are

no connections in life that last. Look at you and Theseus. Theseus is gone. And while you might want to
honor him with this… Commitment, that's about you.
He isn't here. And my relationship with him fractured
years before his death. Nothing lasts forever, Ariadne."

"So what? I should just accept the inherent loneliness of the human condition and wallow in misery?
Sounds like fun."

"No. Just accept that it's all an illusion."

"Then what are we doing here? If all of this, if connection, if care of any kind is an *illusion*, then why are
you here with me?"

He went remote then, his eyes going hard, shutting
her out completely. Then he laughed. "I don't know.
Perhaps there is something in me that doesn't fully believe my own creed. Or perhaps I'm just like so many
other devotees of a religion who follow it imperfectly. I
believe in making your own way. But apparently I can't
entirely let go of the past."

Her breath left her body, her heart pounding hard.
He was admitting to something. To that connection between them, and to the fact that it had never truly been
broken, not by years. Not by that one, heated moment.

She felt undone with it.

She wanted to deny it. Wanted to turn away from it.

But if it was so easy to turn away from Dionysus, she
wouldn't have held the memory of the kiss so close. But
maybe that was part of her problem. Maybe part of the
problem was that no matter how much she might want it

to, her passion couldn't entirely be extinguished. When she had been younger, it had been expressed in the way she had loved to explore the island. And she had connected with Dionysus that way. Then when she'd been sixteen in the water, she had felt it change to something different. Growth. And that frightened her. Because she had already made her bargain. Before she had understood what desire was. And once she did understand, she feared it. Then when she'd been eighteen, he had turned the key that he'd put in the lock two years earlier. He had showed her exactly what she could want. Exactly what she could feel.

And it had changed her. Utterly and completely.

And terrified her. She had doubled down on the decision that she had made.

Because the idea of wanting somebody that way, of trying to build stability that way, was foolish. And she well knew it. Because she had seen the way that her father...

To try and make herself matter to a man by using her body was to make herself disposable.

That brought her back to the moment. To reality.

It underlined the importance of staying on the path. Because as long as she had the company, if she was going to be a mother, then there was security coming from many places.

She was... Useful. She mattered.

And when she looked at Dionysus everything zeroed in on him. Only him. She couldn't allow that.

"I don't know how to look at you now," he said. His words were rough, and she didn't quite understand the note in his voice.

"What do you mean?"

"When I kissed you on the balcony, I thought that I was fighting against the passion you felt for my brother. When you acted shock, as if I might've been Theseus, I assumed that the two of you must have an incendiary connection, and that is how I have always looked at you. I wanted you, Ariadne. But I thought you were giving your body to my brother. With the enthusiasm that you returned my kiss, but you weren't. You felt something for him, but not what I imagine, and now you're telling me... Are you a virgin, Ariadne?"

She felt pinned to the spot. Because exposing Theseus's secrets had meant exposing her own. And perhaps the impossibility of tearing apart Theseus and his secrets was simply too much for Dionysus to bear, and that brought the spotlight straight back to her. She hadn't fully considered that. She felt foolish for that.

And now he was asking...

What did it matter? She had chosen to make sex a non-event in her life. She had chosen to make herself more than desire. So what did it matter?

"Yes," she said.

"God in heaven. That is a travesty."

"It's my choice. If I had wanted to find lovers and make them sign nondisclosure agreements I could've done so. I chose to live my life the way that I have. I have other things that matter more."

"Because you never wanted him," said Dionysus. "Clearly."

"When I thought that I was in love with your brother, I was too young to know what desire felt like. And yes, as I got older, and… No. I didn't want him. Not really."

"Did you want me?"

"I cannot have this conversation with you, Dionysus. I can't. I closed the door on that years ago. And I did it on purpose. I chose a life of stability. A life of safety." And suddenly she felt the dam inside of her beginning to crack, beginning to break. Because she had chosen that life of safety and now it was gone. She had chosen him because it was love in a way she could manage. Could contain it all within her and never wonder if it would betray her.

She had suppressed all of her passion, because she had chosen safety over it. She had… She had allowed herself to feel nothing but shame because of that kiss she had shared with Dionysus, because of what it had made her feel.

She had allowed herself to feel crushed by it.

Because she had wanted that emotional safety he represented above all else.

Now it was gone.

It was gone and she was left with this, this raw, un-filtered emotion. This temptation that had never truly gone away.

What a fool she had been.

The world wasn't safe. Her choices hadn't kept her safe because how could they? Her friendship, her marriage had insulated her but now that it was gone everything she'd never dealt with had been dragged out into the light. Exposed.

It was all still there, unhealed and unmanaged. And she was angry. At herself most of all for not seeing that someday a reckoning would come. Even if Theseus had lived it would have come. They would have divorced and she would no longer have had their marriage to shield her from the choices she'd tried to stop herself from ever having to make.

They were still there.

And so was Dionysus.

She stood then, and so did he.

"I didn't want to be disposable. I don't want to be… out here unsafe and unprotected in the world without…him." She finished that on a fierce whisper. She looked at him, and suddenly, it was like the veil had been ripped away. Like that crumbling dam had let forth not just the grief, but the need that she had been suppressing every time she looked at him, not just these past weeks, but every time she had looked at him since she was sixteen years old.

That gala where he'd goaded her about stealing champagne and swimming in fountains.

Christmas, three years ago, when they'd found themselves alone at the bar adjacent to the dining room at her and Theseus's stately London home.

I won't ask if you're getting champagne.

He was teasing her and it was welcome. It had been a long time. She tried to ignore the tangle of feelings in her heart.

She wasn't supposed to have feelings for him at all.

That kiss wasn't supposed to be the first thing she thought of when she saw his face.

It had been years.

They had never spoken of it again.

They didn't have to.

I like champagne, she said.

These days I prefer something harder, but perhaps you can toast to our youth.

Or four years ago, when they'd both gone to a political event in London and had been forced to sit through droning speeches. Their eyes had caught across the room and held.

He didn't smile, but the light in his eyes reminded her of when he was younger. And by the time it was over her guard was down and she found herself standing in a corridor with him, hiding from everyone else as they talked about nothing as substantial even as the weather, but she felt consumed by it. Cocooned.

She forgot she was married until she saw her ring flashing in the light.

Then she'd had to leave. She'd barely said goodbye. She'd needed space. To think. To breathe.

Then she thought back to six years ago at Easter Brunch when he'd wound up all the small children with sweets and had turned them feral before the egg hunt had begun.

She'd admonished him—but none of the children were hers so it had been amusing more than anything.

Don't you wish we'd had that sort of fun as kids?

We did.

Her breath froze in her chest. She thought he might be remembering the kiss.

Not when we were this small.

Or at her wedding, when she'd avoided him entirely. He'd been the best man, but the tension had been thick. She'd blamed the anger between him and Theseus over the kiss. And not her own feelings.

Then there was ten years ago…

He'd been coming right to her. And she'd let him.

He wrapped his arms around her, his hold strong. And when he lowered his head and claimed her mouth, it was like she had been dipped in the living flame.

She wanted to be burned.

She wanted to forget.

It was like jumping from high rocks into the sea. It was like climbing to the top of a mountain.

It was like running, barefoot and without a care across the sand.

It was the full expression of all the wildness that lived in her soul. And for a brief, shining moment she embraced it as she let him embrace her. As she felt the slide of his tongue against hers. And then echo of salvation rang throughout her body.

What the hell is going on?

And then she was back. Back in the moment. Looking at the man seated before her. And she wanted… She wanted to go back. She wanted to have that kiss. She wanted to feel passion. Because turning away from it hadn't protected her.

She had devoted herself to someone else's life.

She had promised her body to that marriage, like a nun to the church, as she'd often thought.

Even though she hadn't ever had sex. She had traded that part of herself away, and she had done it for a reason, but that reason had turned out to mean nothing.

Nothing. She had been left anyway.

She hadn't been enough anyway.

And there she was, staring at the man that she had wanted. Oh, he would've broken her several times over by now.

He would never love her. He didn't believe in that sort of love, and neither did she. Why should they? Why should they? They had never been shown an ounce of it in their own lives.

But she wanted him.

She wanted him, and the real reason that she had to keep her distance from him was that it had never gone away.

She wanted to weep. But she wasn't going to. Because she wasn't going to collapse.

"Yes," she said again, stronger this time. "I am a virgin."

"A shame," he said.

His words were casual, but his tone wasn't. He sounded harsh. Hoarse. As if speaking them had been a struggle.

And suddenly, she felt like she was being weighed down by the burden of her virginity. And she had kept it all these years and for what?

She had turned off that part of herself for what?

Dionysus had wanted her once. And rather than diving into it headfirst, she had turned away from it. She had never spoken of it, she hadn't even allowed herself to think of it. Not honestly. Yes, she had decided internally, that she had thought it was Theseus, but not to absolve herself so much as to protect herself. From the truth of it. From the deep, resonant reality of it all.

The fact that she wasn't effortlessly free of the temptations of her father or the women who got themselves tangled up with him. The sins of her mother, no.

She was simply very, very good at hiding. Very good at being afraid. And she had still ended up alone.

So it was all for nothing.

She had stolen it from herself for nothing.

Theseus had stood between herself and Dionysus all these years. And now he was gone.

It was an entanglement she didn't need.

It was one she didn't want.

It was one she should turn away from.

"Dionysus," she said. "Kiss me."

CHAPTER EIGHT

EVERYTHING IN HIM went still. The revelations of the past twenty minutes had taken everything he believed and turned them on its head.

His brother hadn't been in love with Ariadne. And he had married her all the same.

His brother hadn't *wanted* Ariadne, and he had claimed her nonetheless.

But he had never touched her.

Dionysus had waited for her.

He could still remember the agony of realization that she hadn't done the same for him.

That he had never given in to any sort of sexual temptation because there was nothing greater than his desire for her. But he had simply been waiting for her to be ready. For her to want him.

And then… And then he had found out they were engaged. Nothing matched that. The anger that he had felt. The brutality of it.

The realization that Ariadne had given her body to Theseus.

A man identical to him in every way physically.

He had not been rejected because of his body, but because of who he was. And that was like dying.

And yet, it hadn't been that. Not ever.

But he would not give her what she wanted just because she demanded it. Because she tried to absolve herself here. To make it so the move had to be his.

He burned with anger. At himself, at his brother. At her. He ached with grief. Fresh and new, because his brother had lived in a hell that he hadn't even realized he was in. Because he wanted to shake Theseus and tell him there was no shame in who he had been made to be. And he had never been given that chance. Because of his forbidden desire for Ariadne.

But it was all a circle, because if Theseus hadn't lied to him, then...

They could have figured something else out.

But he had lied. He had shown all the world that Ariadne belonged to him, when all she had been was a shield. His protection.

He knew his brother had experienced pain. He knew Ariadne had been more than a shield, but a dear friend, but they were both still left with all this. This shattered, ruined world.

And now she was alone.

But he had been soft with her all these weeks.

And her grief was not even that which he had thought. It was something else.

The loss of a friendship, the loss of her stability.

The potential loss of her inheritance, but not the loss of her lover.

She had never had a lover.

Mine.

And that was when he realized, there was no question about any of this going forward.

There would be no artificial insemination. He would make her his. In every way. And, however she wanted to pass the baby off... Whatever lies she wanted to tell his father, she could do so. But the child would know the truth, and so would he.

She would be his. There was no question.

Possibility was a roaring beast inside of him. A possibility that hadn't existed only moments ago.

And all the dangers remained.

He couldn't love her, not in the way she deserved. But neither had Theseus. So why couldn't he have her, imperfectly.

Why not?

"Tell me," he said. "Did you really believe that I was my brother?"

"No," she said.

"And why did you lie?"

"Because... Because I was afraid. I was afraid of what that meant."

"When you were sixteen, and we went swimming together. You wanted to kiss me," he said.

"Yes," she whispered.

"You were afraid."

"Yes. I was afraid. Because you could have made me go back on my word. You could've made me… I'm not a fool, Dionysus. I knew that it wasn't love. I have never seen any evidence in my life that romantic love exists or means anything. And all I wanted was something stable. Something safe. I knew that with you it could be… Mad and passionate and dangerous."

"It still could be," he said. "I've wanted you for a long time. Don't you understand that something like this could set us both on fire?"

"Yes," she said, her voice a hushed whisper.

"And?"

"I tried the other way. I tried, and what did I get for it? *Nothing*. I am left here fighting by myself. I am left with the awful realization that whatever I've tried has never been sufficient enough to protect me. I would rather have what I want and damn the consequences."

"Little girl, don't you know that I will devour you?" Need roared in his veins, his whole body on high alert.

"Yes," she whispered.

"Then so be it."

He moved toward her, his heart thundering hard. She sat there, looking up at him, and then she stood, moving down the table, the dress poured over her curves like liquid. Her eyes glittered, and he growled.

Because he had wanted her, and he had kept himself on this leash. Had martyred himself to this desire for so long, and now she was offering herself to him.

"How many men have you kissed?"

"You and Theseus," she said.

"Did you ever kiss him because you wanted him?"

She shook her head. "It was a performance. Every time." She swallowed. "I admit that I felt attraction to him, but..." She looked down. "It was a shadow of what I felt for you. And that was why I liked it. Theseus needed me. I was his support, his confidante. You... You didn't need me at all. You were wild and untamed, and you whipped up the wildness in me. I was afraid of that. It was much better to be needed. It was much better to be the one who was necessary."

"You wanted me?"

"I didn't know what it was at first. I didn't understand. I was too young. But when you kissed me I did. And I knew that I couldn't... I knew that I couldn't. And he would never have married me if he knew that I wanted you."

"I don't think that's true. He was desperate from the sounds of things."

"Yes, but so was I. To feel secure and he offered me...he offered me stability. A commitment to our friendship that was so deep and I wanted it. It was my choice."

"As you said. A choice you made when you were a girl. So you tell me now, what choice is it that you make as a woman?"

She understood. But it was up to her. That she was going to have to close the distance between them. Because he had done it once already. And he had paid for it.

She moved toward him, and something like a fist tightened in his chest. She was so beautiful. Her dark hair, her glittering eyes. And the woman standing in front of him right now, she was the one who ran over the island with him. She was the one who made everything brighter.

She was the one he desired. Above all else.

She wrapped her arms around his neck, their mouths a whisper apart.

An echo of the swim they had taken the other day. An echo of the desire they felt in their youth.

And then finally, she pressed her soft lips against his. And that was all the invitation he needed. He growled, crushing her lips to his, and forcing them apart, because he was starving, and he had waited enough time.

His heart was raging, his body hard as steel.

He wanted her. Desperately.

Needed her. With a strength that transcended anything else.

He felt nothing but desire. And it was like the past decade had burned away. Like he was twenty years old again, claiming her mouth finally. His body untried, preserved for her. Only for her.

He wanted this woman. With everything in him. He wanted her.

And she would be his. Because Theseus hadn't touched her.

Untouched.

His.

His arousal surged, his whole body alight with need.

"I aim to have you in every way possible," he said. "I would've had you that night, you know."

She shivered. Her need apparent as she did so.

Yes. She needed this just as badly as he did.

He cupped her face, letting his fingers drift over her lovely, familiar features. She had been there, within arm's reach for all these years, and yet utterly untouchable. Behind glass. And that was how his brother had kept her. A doll that he had put in a box, treated like a collector's item and placed on the shelf. Untouched. Virginal.

In pristine condition.

He intended to ruin her. Utterly. In the way that she had ruined him all those years ago. It wasn't vengeance, no. It was a reckoning.

For the unutterable need within him demanded satisfaction, and it would have it now.

And she would burn the way that he had.

She trembled. He relished it.

He thought of how he had been the first time he kissed her. Trembling himself. Wild with the risk he was taking, and with all the need in his veins.

He had been eager, untried like a horse.

And now, he knew exactly how to touch a woman. Exactly how to prolong pleasure. To turn it into agony.

He intended to do so with her. Tonight.

On her birthday.

He moved his hands down her neck, let his fingertips drift along her collarbone, flicking the strap of her dress away from her shoulder. He could see her nipples bead beneath the thin fabric. She couldn't be wearing a bra with this dress. Her breasts were perfect. He already knew they would fill his palms just so. Round and firm. His mouth watered. He wanted them in his mouth. He wanted to taste her. Yes. He wanted her.

He did his best to hold his need at bay. To keep control. He had practice restraining himself, as long as he wasn't touching her. But now that he was…

He drew the front of her dress down, exposing one perfectly rounded breast, and a dusky colored nipple.

She was beautiful. Beyond. A goddess.

He had seen countless women naked. But it had never been Ariadne, so it didn't matter.

Mine.

Her breath left her body in a gust, and he savored the reaction. The obvious need on her face.

"Take your clothes off for me," he said.

Would she fight against him or would she obey. He wasn't certain. But then with trembling hands she unzipped her dress, and let it fall to her hips, then she slipped out of it, her eyes round, her lips parted, her breath escaping in short bursts. She was standing there in only a pair of very brief underwear the same color as the dress. And a pair of shocking pink heels.

"Beautiful," he said. "I want to see everything."

She took her shoes off, and he thought about demanding she leave them on, but decided he didn't need that kind of performance. He just needed Ariadne. Soft and pliant and his.

Then she took her underwear off, and his eyes zeroed in on the dark thatch of curls between her legs.

He felt like his skin was being flayed away from his bones.

He had never felt desire this sharp. This acute. It had never mattered so much who he was looking at. It was Ariadne's skin.

Ariadne's secrets.

All for him.

He was never possessive, not with anyone but her.

And living with the agony of not possessing that which he wanted to be only his was something he had become accustomed to living with. A wound he knew would never heal, but was his all the same.

And now…

It was like healing and being cut all at the same time.

He moved to her, and lifted her up, gripping her thighs and encouraging her to wrap her legs around his waist. He claimed her mouth, holding the back of her head as he did so, feeling her breasts crushed against his chest.

He wrenched his mouth away from her, his arm around her waist as he walked them both out of the dining room and up the stairs.

He took her into his room.

It was dark, nearly empty. With windows that gave them a view of the sea. But that didn't matter. The only view he needed was her.

She gasped as he threw her down on the bed, gazing at her as she lay there with her legs slightly parted.

"Yes," he growled. "Open your legs for me."

Color flooded her cheeks.

Yes. She was a virgin. It was so hard for him to remember that.

And yet, that stamp of possessiveness had branded itself upon his soul.

She was his. Only his, and while he knew it, he could also scarcely believe that a woman so beautiful was untouched. But it was there, written in that flush on her cheeks, and her hesitance now.

"I think you're beautiful," he said. "And I want to see all of you."

"I… I don't think I can."

"Let me help," he said.

He moved onto the bed, and pressed his palms to the insides of both thighs, parting her legs and giving himself a perfect view of her glistening, pink flesh.

She was wet. For him.

"Yes," he growled. He moved his hand, up the inside of her thigh, just to the edge of that tempting glory there. And he paused. To say a prayer. Because he was about to tread on holy ground. He had dreamed of this.

Of her. Before he could even imagine how glorious it would be.

But now he knew.

He slid his finger through her slick folds, before moving down to push one inside of her.

She gasped, her hips lifting up off the bed.

"I'll take it slow," he said.

She bit her lip, moving her hips in a sinuous rhythm. "I... I've had... I doubt there's a barrier still."

Of course. She had medical procedures that would've probably dealt with that.

"But you are still a virgin," he said.

The word echoed inside of him. He had known that it mattered to him back then. Because it had mattered in the way that he had deferred his own pleasure for her.

He hadn't realized it could possibly matter now.

It did.

He moved his thumb over that sensitive bundle of nerves there, as he pushed one finger in and out of her body, before adding another, watching as her expression transformed into one of pleasure. Feeling her thighs relax, as she began to lose track of her shame.

Then he bent down, and replaced his thumb with his tongue, tasting her sweetness. Ariadne.

He withdrew his fingers and gripped her hips, pulling her forward, claiming her with his mouth. He growled against her, lapping at her skin, unable to stop himself from devouring her entirely. This was his fantasy. Her. This.

And when she shattered beneath his touch, he consumed every drop of her desire, his body pulsing with need.

But he wanted it to last.

He had waited for ten years.

And this night would take as long as he wanted it to.

Ariadne was undone.

She was boneless, panting. And Dionysus was above her like a dark god, lord of the underworld, staring down at her with sharp eyes. He was still fully clothed, and it made her ashamed of just how hard she had shattered.

But he was… He was not unaffected.

Sweat beaded on his brow, and he breathed heavily.

And the hunger in his eyes was unmatched. Undeniable.

"Take your clothes off," she said, repetition of what he had said to her.

A look of triumph crossed his face as he got off the bed and began to unbutton his shirt.

Her mouth dried as he exposed that gorgeous chest, those beautiful muscles. She had seen him shirtless only recently, but not like this. Not knowing that she was going to be able to touch him. To taste him like he had tasted her, if she wanted to.

And she did.

She had tried so hard to suppress this part of herself. Had been ashamed of it.

But she refused to be ashamed of it now.

She wanted him.

She wanted Dionysus.

She always had.

And she was going to have him.

He had just licked her like she was ice cream, and it left her shaken.

But in the best way.

And the only thing she could think, as he shrugged his shirt off his shoulders, and his hand went to his belt, was that the one good thing about being alone in life as she was, was that no one was around to be ashamed of her. There was no one to perform for. Nobody to please. It was all about pleasing herself. Keeping herself safe.

But no one else would ever even have to know about this.

It was all for her. All her need. All her desire.

He removed the rest of his clothes, and then she was looking at a naked man in person for the first time in her life.

She was very afraid that what she had done was open Pandora's box. Because the need inside of her was as keen as if she hadn't just experienced a shattering climax.

She'd had orgasms before, of course.

She was familiar with her own body. But there was always regret attached to it. She wished she didn't need the release. She wished that she could be as free of temptation as she pretended that she was.

And if she saw Dionysus's face sometimes when she reached climax, she had told herself that it was more Theseus, because it had to do with her familiarity with him. He was the man she knew best after all.

But if she was honest, she knew that it was Dionysus she was thinking about all this time.

As ever.

She let her gaze drop to his arousal. Bronzed and hard, standing out proud from his body. Thick and glorious. She chased that feeling of knowing that there was nobody to disappoint. That the only person she would ever be accountable to for this was herself.

And if she didn't enjoy it to the fullest, she would have herself to answer to. And so, she pushed aside any virginal nerves and got up onto her knees, moving toward him. She tentatively wrapped her hand around his arousal, squeezing him.

"You're beautiful," she said. Just as he had said to her. His teeth were pressed tight together, his breath exiting his mouth on a hard hiss. Her mouth watered when she looked at him, and she leaned in, flicking her tongue over the crown of him. Then she wrapped her lips around him and took him as deep as she could.

His response was nearly violent. He reached back and grabbed a handful of her hair, tugging hard.

She looked up at him. "Did I do something wrong?"

"No," he growled. "Don't stop."

She moved back to him, taking him in deeper, sliding her tongue over that hot, satiny flesh.

He tasted incredible. Dionysus.

The one man she had ever wanted like this. With a burning passion that would have left her ashamed at one time.

It had left her ashamed.

But not now.

She pleasured him like that until he gripped her hair again, moving her away. "I don't want to finish like that."

The image that painted was erotic.

She did want him to finish like that.

She wanted to swallow him down. To have all of him. To feel wanted. Suddenly, she felt a surge in her chest, power like she had never known.

She had imagined that desire left women weak. But she had never fully understood how powerful it could make a woman feel. She felt powerful. Because he wanted her. Wanted her so badly he was shaking with it. Wanted her so badly that he could no longer allow her to pleasure him with her mouth. Because he would lose control. Utterly.

He wanted her. And that mattered.

He wanted her, and that made her powerful.

Still, she obeyed him, patiently waiting to find out what would happen next. She ached for him. And when he moved back to her, and kissed her mouth, taking her deep and long, she sighed against him, her hands on his broad chest, moving over his muscles, the hair on his chest was crisp and enticing, his skin hot. She marveled at the difference in texture touching him versus touching herself.

He was so masculine. Absolute perfection. Large where she was small. Hard where she was soft.

He held her tightly, her breasts crushed to his chest, his hard abdomen like steel against her much softer body.

And then she felt that ridge of his arousal, and she wanted to guide him where she needed him most. She ached for him. She felt empty.

She was so wet it would've been embarrassing, if it hadn't felt so good. Her body was ready for him.

"Please," she whispered.

"I'm not going to wear a condom," he said against her mouth.

They were close. Close to the time when her doctor had said they could try to conceive.

It made her want to weep. The idea that their baby could be conceived tonight. This way.

She felt like she wasn't entirely prepared for that. Like it made it more real. How could she ask him to release his claim on a child that they had made in bed together?

She wanted to ask him that. But she couldn't make the words come out. Because she wanted him. Bare and without a barrier inside of her.

So she pushed all of her reservations away.

"Yes," she said.

He pushed her down onto her back and hooked her

leg up over his hip. Then he guided himself toward the entrance of her body, sliding in slowly. He was so big, she felt her body stretch to accommodate him. She might not have a barrier remaining, but she had still never been tested like this. It felt good. So good, to have him fill her like this, even as it almost felt like too much.

"Dionysus," she said, his name a prayer on her lips.

And then he began to move, hard and intense, a feral growl on his lips every time he thrust back home within her. She came alive. Like she had never truly known joy until this moment. Like she hadn't been a whole person. How had she walked on this earth for twenty-eight years without knowing what it was like to have a man inside of her. Without knowing what it was like to have Dionysus inside of her. She had thought to give this away. To give it up for safety, and safety was an illusion.

This was worth all the risks. This was worth everything.

She said his name like an incantation, over and over again as he claimed her. She looked up at his face, they really weren't identical. It was always so clear who was who. Dionysus was wild. And never more so than now. His dark eyes gleamed, his lip curled, his teeth like those of a predator, glinting in the dark light.

She wanted him. She had him, and yet she felt like it wasn't enough. He was deep within her, and yet she wanted to be closer. She moved her hands over his shoulders, let her fingernails dig into his flesh. She cried out with her need, her need to be filled, her need for release. Her need for this to never end. Never.

She wrapped her legs around his waist, trying to take him deeper, deeper still. Arching her hips against his. Their skin was slick with sweat, the sounds they made untamed.

Finally. Finally.

She didn't feel virginal, not now.

Because she felt as if she had been building to this moment all of her life. Like everything had been waiting for this. Poised on the edge.

And when he found his release, she went right over the edge with him, shattering as he spilled himself within her, his hardness pulsing inside. She gripped him, taking him deeper, deeper as she cried out his name.

And then it was done. Except… With her heart beating hard, lying there exhausted but not sated, she knew that it wasn't done. She knew that it couldn't be. It would take more than once. More than a night.

This need couldn't be satisfied quite so easily.

"Ariadne."

He leaned in and kissed her. It was tender. So different than everything else had been. And she let her need to embrace that tenderness wash through her.

His lips were like home.

And it made her want to weep.

This moment… This was all she had ever wanted. The way that he held her was so strong and firm and sure.

It was everything. And so was he.

He moved away from her then, rolling onto his back. "You realize this changes things."

It was like being doused with cold water. "Does it?"

"Of course it does. There is no question now of artificial insemination. You and I don't need the intervention of a doctor in order to conceive a child."

She put her hand on her stomach.

She felt… Wounded. Confused by the abrupt shift.

"Is that all you wanted?" she asked, "the chance to avoid having to do it into a cup?"

"Of course not," he said. "But there is nothing standing between us now. I wasn't going to touch you out of deference to my brother, and out of deference to your loss. But now that I know the truth of it… You're mine, Ariadne. I will allow you to pass my baby off as my brother's. But only to my father. And when he dies, the world will know the truth. But by then it won't matter anyway. Because you will be my wife."

"What?"

"You're going to marry me, Ariadne. Because you're mine. And I'm going to make sure that everyone knows that."

CHAPTER NINE

EVERYTHING HAD BECOME clear to him the moment he had buried himself deep inside of her.

She was his.

There was no question, there was no hesitation. Once he had claimed her, he would never go back to not having her.

"Your father will appreciate that," she said, turning away from him.

He gripped her arm, and didn't let her scamper across the room. "Are you implying that I only did this to try and secure access to the company? To try and secure some sort of approval from my father? Have you listened to nothing that I've said to you." Rage was a living flame in his chest. But then, it always was.

"I don't know," she said.

"Understand one thing, Ariadne. I have wanted you from the first moment I knew how a man could be with a woman. As certain as my brother ever was about his desires, mine were just as fixed. It was you. Why do you think I kissed you even knowing you were engaged to my brother? Why do you think I risked the spectacle?

Because there was no risk. I either had you or I didn't, and everything else was collateral damage. The only reason I didn't steal you away is that you didn't seem as if you wanted to go. I want you. I am also realistic enough to know that I would have destroyed us at least seven hundred different ways by now. I do not regret the way of things. I can't. But you are mine now. After all this time, and if you think that has anything to do with money, or pleasing anyone but myself, then you are a fool."

He released his hold on her.

"If you want me so much then why can't you be civil for five blessed seconds?"

"Because there is nothing simple about desire like this. It has teeth. If you don't understand that…"

She stood up, and he was overwhelmed by the sight of her naked body. He had seen countless women. They didn't matter. Nothing mattered but her.

His sexuality had belonged to her from the first. He had not been lying or exaggerating when he'd said that.

But he also wanted her to be clear not to confuse that with softer, more refined feelings.

Theseus hadn't felt passion for her, apparently. He felt nothing but passion for her.

And when he said that it was painful, he did not lie.

If he was a better man it might bother him that she didn't feel the same. Or it might deter him. He wished that she did. He wished that she would burn right along with him.

"I have never been free, Dionysus. I married your brother when I was so young. And I committed myself to it long before we walked down the aisle. You're asking me to chain myself to another man."

"And one who looks just like the other one. People will think you have no imagination."

"Stop it. You're nothing like him. You've never been identical, not to me. I lied. I lied the night that you kissed me. Not just to Theseus, but to myself. I wanted to think that I imagined it was him. I didn't. I knew that it was you, and I hated it. It terrified me. I never wanted… I don't want this," she said. "It hurts, you're right."

The beast within him was gratified to hear her say that.

"I have pushed it down, and pushed down all this time. All this time, Dionysus, because I was afraid that if I let it out I would… Am I my father? Or am I his endless succession of lovers, who can say? And I don't like either one. I have never seen lust dressed up as romantic love become anything other than a weapon. You either destroy people with it or are destroyed by it, and I don't want it. I chose what I thought was safer. I chose what felt…you just can't be safe in this world, can you?"

"Perhaps not," he said. "But I won't leave. You have my word on that. If I could have let go of my need for you, then I would have done it a long time ago."

"You sleep with women interchangeably. How could you possibly say that just because you're attracted to me, and that attraction has endured, that you have experienced any kind of…"

"I was a virgin the night that I kissed you," he said. "I wanted you. I didn't want sex. When it became clear that I would never have you I gorged myself on sex. To prove to myself that it didn't need to be you, to prove to myself that it didn't have to mean anything. I have had all the partners that I could ever care to have. It didn't take it away, Ariadne. Nothing did. I wanted you all the same, every time I saw you."

It was his turn to stand, and he began to pace the length of the room. "You, my brother's perfect wife. So buttoned up, so demure. You have any idea how badly I wanted to wreck that façade? Do you have any idea how badly I wanted to… I thought about it. Kissing you, in your own home. With your husband in the very next room, I thought about it. I thought about violating your marriage vows in a hundred different ways, because I wanted to rid myself of that demon. Don't tell me what I want. Don't tell me what will fade. Do not try to minimize what I have felt for you because I chose a way to handle my solitude in a fashion you can't quite understand."

She shifted, her breasts moving along with her, and he couldn't help but let his eyes drop down to their perfection.

"We don't know each other," she said. "Not anymore. I'm not certain we ever did. You thought all this time that I was in love with your brother. That I was… His lover, and I wasn't. And I thought... I thought the kiss was a game to you."

"Then you're right," he said. "We never knew each other. I thought we did. I thought here, in this place, you knew me in a way that nobody else did."

"Did you love me, Dionysus?"

The words cut him like a knife.

"I thought I did. Yes. I got over it."

"You just never got over the desire to see me naked?"

"What I got over was the idea that life might be a fairy tale. I was tempted to believe it when I met you. Because you were... Something bright in what had been darkness until that very moment. So yes, I thought it was love. It was the first blush of lust, and I didn't know better. I stayed a virgin until I was twenty years old because of how badly I wanted you. I told myself that had to be true love, because what else could it be? But you are right. I also have never seen any evidence of romantic love being anything other than painful. Anything other than a shifting tide. Lust, that's honest. The things that our body say that we want, that's real. But it is a hunger like any other. And perhaps like your love of chocolate cake, my desire for you is simply innate. A preference. One that I couldn't change if I tried. It will always be the thing that I want the most. But that is not love."

"You don't believe in love?"

"No. Not in any fashion. Life is a series of bonds that can be broken always. Depending on which angle you come at them from. I was a twin, Ariadne, there is no longer bond. I was formed in the womb with my brother, and in the end, we didn't trust one another. I felt betrayed by him when he took you, even though he could not have known that I wanted you for myself. I didn't tell him. I held back. Then I kissed you, and he felt like that was a betrayal, when to me it felt like being true to myself. But he was harboring his own secrets, and he didn't tell me the truth. I would have said that bond was the closest thing to love, but was it? To have been given a brother that close, so close we even share facial features. And to not even be able to maintain that, that says more about Theseus and myself than anything else ever could."

She was silent then, staring at him. "How do you see the marriage, then?"

"I will support you. As you run the business. I will be a role model to our child. You can tell my father whatever you need to. It doesn't matter to me. As long as we know. You had a marriage based on friendship with Theseus, why should we be different?"

Because they were never really friends. They had been something different. He knew that. But maybe she didn't feel it. And maybe she wouldn't admit it now.

Even if she had.

"You will be faithful to me?"

"Of course. Have you listened to nothing that I've said?"

"I just find it hard to believe. You have seemed utterly uninterested in me these past years, and now you're telling me… I don't know how to look at you." She repeated his own words back to him.

"You and I are both filled with secrets. We will have to start over."

She nodded. "Yes. I would… I feel that we should wait to marry. An appropriate amount of time. We should wait until after the baby is born."

"The baby we have yet to conceive?"

In spite of himself, he felt his body begin to harden again, at the mention of working to conceive a baby.

She was ruinous to him.

"You think in that way we can create a narrative that will make it appear as if we simply… Fell for one another in the absence of your husband?"

"Well, it's better than making it look as if I jumped into your bed immediately following his death."

"You did, though."

"But I was never in his bed. Which you now know."

"I don't understand why the two of you didn't carry on affairs," he said.

She blinked. "I told you. What I wanted was to be safe. I wanted security. I didn't want all of the dangerous things that came with passion. Not in the least. What I wanted was to have… I wanted to have safety. He was my safety. He was… He was meant to be everything. He would give me a home, he would give me a family, he would give me a baby. And he was my friend."

"And that was enough for you."

"It was. It was until it wasn't enough for him anymore. It was hard to watch him struggle but he did find love. It wasn't going to be forever but at that point I trusted that I wouldn't lose him even if we divorced. We were making a family together. I was supposed to have that."

"And now you have me," he said, somewhat ruefully.

She met his gaze. "I knew exactly what being married to Theseus would look like. He was very clear on it. There was not going to be any sex. In private we were best friends and in public we played our roles expertly. I knew exactly what it would look like, I could imagine it clearly even when I was younger. But I can't imagine marriage to you."

"More of this," he said.

She looked away, her cheeks turning pink. "I'm having a hard time embracing this is something... Something it's okay for me to want."

"Here is what I can promise you. And don't dismiss me this time. I will never trade you in for anyone or anything else. When I make vows I keep them. And I protect what's mine. There is no greater truth than that."

She moved closer to him, and his heart froze in his chest. Then she reached out and put her hand just there, over where his heart had ceased beating. And it started again.

"I'm tired of being lonely."

Her words hit him strangely. Loneliness was simply part of life. At least, as far as he could see. As far as he could understand it. He didn't know if there was any real way to fix that. Except when she touched him, he felt something quiet inside of him. He felt like he could breathe.

As if he was drawing a full breath for the first time in many years.

She leaned in and pressed her mouth to his. It was slow, achingly deliberate. There was no mistaking that she had chosen this. No mistaking that she meant to kiss him.

And when she pulled away, her green eyes were shining. "Yes, Dionysus. I'll marry you."

CHAPTER TEN

SHE WAS WRUNG OUT. She was… On the edge of herself. But the truth was, she was bound to Dionysus whether she married him or not. If they had a baby… He was right. She had been fooling herself. Thinking that it would be so simple as to have his baby and pretend… And pretend. Even when she had first thought of carrying his child instead of Theseus's she had felt the weight of that intimacy. Even before they had made love.

And now… She knew that she would never be able to pretend the child belonged to Theseus. Not forever.

She could lie to her father-in-law, but she could never lie to the child. She would never be able to cut Dionysus out of this.

She suddenly felt… Overcome with shame. What she had asked of him was deeply selfish. It had been on behalf of Theseus, but… Had it been?

Had she only been trying to justify her own decisions?

That was entirely possible.

Trying to prove that she had been relevant in some

way. Was that what all of this was about? She wondered. She really did.

And the truth was, she wanted him.

If she hadn't, she wouldn't have been able to give herself to him like this. She had always wanted him. She had been scared. And then a few moments ago she had managed to be angry enough to push that fear aside. And now she was...

Ashamed. Of her own behavior. Ashamed of how she had used Dionysus as a convenient object.

In a bid to avoid seeing him as a man.

There was no denying he was a man now. He sat there next to her, a perfect sculpture. His well muscled shoulders and arms a testament to his strength. His chest was broad, his waist tapered and solid. His thighs were thick and well defined, and that most masculine part of him was beginning to rouse again, so quickly after they had already come together.

She was sore, but she would take him again.

All these years...

It was tempting to believe that this was fate. But... None of this felt like fate. Because it had taken the death of Theseus, and the loss of her pregnancy for her to be here.

And those things could simply never feel meant to be. Perhaps that was what people told themselves when they were desperate to dress their lust up to something other than that basest of needs.

Perhaps that was why.

She couldn't readily untangle what they were. But she felt good when she kissed him.

And she wanted more.

"Why do you want to marry me?"

"You asked. Or rather, you told me to."

He chuckled. "Is that all, sweet Ariadne? Is that all I ever had to do? Crook my finger and make demands of you and you would come?"

He let the double entendre linger between them, she was certain that he meant it.

"I don't want to be without you," she said.

And that was true.

Real enough at least.

"Do you want me, or do you want the connection to my family?"

"I already have Katrakis Shipping. I have a connection to your family."

But she couldn't deny that his words got under her skin like the edge of a knife's blade.

"And you're right. About the baby. I wanted to give Theseus something that he didn't get the chance to have. I don't need to do that. Life can be cruel in some ways, but... I can't right that wrong by enacting another wrong. Our child will know his father. And that will be you."

"Good."

"You said, though, that you didn't want a child."

"I never have. It turns out, though, that I would love to make one with you."

"There is the making, but then there's the raising."

"I don't know how to do that," he said. "But you don't either."

"No. I don't. We can learn. Together. Our child will be…" She lost herself then, because Theseus and Dionysus were not the same man. She knew it. But she had been lying to herself while she tried desperately to repair the situation she found herself in. And part of that life had been that because they were genetically indistinguishable from one another, the child would be the same as if he had come from Theseus.

But Dionysus was an entirely different man.

Dionysus called to the wildness in her. Together they were something different. Entirely.

"I will need you to help me raise that child," she said. "Because you and I…"

She felt it again, that sensation she had when they had first arrived here on the island. That tapestry of memory. Not a single moment, but a feeling. The essence of what they were. The freedom they had found together.

Their first time together just now had been intense. Of course it had been. But suddenly she wanted more.

"Take me swimming," she said.

He stood up off the bed and held his hand out toward hers, and she took it wordlessly. Slipping off into the night with him.

He knew the path by heart, and she trusted him.

He held her against his body, and then jumped. Then

both of them went into the water, and they surfaced again, breathless, clinging to each other.

He kissed her, deep and long, wildly. They had nearly done this all those years ago. They had nearly done this yesterday.

And now, it was like the culmination of that need, of those moments, all coming together.

They were fire.

They were inevitable.

Except, they very nearly hadn't been at all.

Because she had been afraid.

She had very nearly sacrificed everything to that fear.

Their skin was slick, and he moved his hands over her curves, driving her forward in a frenzy.

To be touched like this, held like this, it was the single most incredible feeling that she could possibly think of.

To be held. To be wanted.

She let layers of her fear fall away.

She had never let herself want this. But she did.

She wanted it down to the very depths of her soul.

She wanted this and him and everything.

Her heart beat fiercely, desperately. Dionysus.

She would never mistake him.

"Dionysus," she said it out loud. Like a prayer, an incantation. A plea for him to never disappear.

And he devoured her. Just as he had promised. Consumed her, left her aching and needy down to her very core. To her essence.

She clung to him, wrapping her legs around his hips, as he hauled them both up out of the water, and laid her down on the sandy shore.

"I always knew you were the enchanted thing here," he said. "When I bought the island, I tried to recapture the magic. I did my very best. And it… It suits me. But it has never been magic. Not since we were here."

Suddenly, she felt overwhelmed. By the truth between them. The reality of what they could've been.

She had asked him if he loved her.

He had.

Had she loved him too? Had she clung to Theseus because he was easier.

Because he represented safety, while Dionysus was the unknown. He still was.

But she had tried safety, and it had gotten her nothing.

And now she was wholly consumed by him.

She wrapped her legs around his hips and canted them upward, urging him to claim her. To take her.

"Good girl," he whispered against her mouth as he thrust his hips forward, in one slick glide, claiming her with his mouth, his hands, his iron masculinity.

She moved against him, chasing release. But chasing something even more dear, that connection that she had felt only ever with him.

And as he moved, the years fell away. As they clung to one another, they were all there was.

And she let him drive them both over the edge.

Their cries filled the night air. He was right.

They were the magic.

And this place was theirs.

She sat up afterward, brushed at some of the sand on her skin. Leaned in and kissed his shoulder before leaning her head against it. They sat like that, saying nothing. She moved her fingertips over his chest, relishing the feel of him. The way that she could touch him. She was trembling. Because the enormity of this moment was blooming inside of her and growing larger and larger, a chasm of desire that she could not entirely rationalize.

She had been dishonest with herself, that was the thing. For so much of this time, she hadn't allowed herself to fully see, to fully know exactly what he meant to her. She had suppressed it, pushed it aside.

And now she wanted to mourn for entirely different reasons.

For the fact that they could have known each other, and hadn't. For the fact they had wasted all these years.

Maybe it wasn't love. Maybe he was right.

But then what was it? She couldn't rightly say.

It was far too difficult to know.

"I will buy you a ring as soon as possible."

"It can't be public," she said, hating herself for saying it, because this was supposed to be their moment.

Because it was supposed to be them, only them, here in this sacred place. And not logistics and machinations, and all the things they had to do because of his father.

His father.

All of this was because of him.

This whole mess.

No. Much of it is because of you.

The realization stung. But it was true. Her own cowardice was not a small part of the mess that had been made here.

"I'm going to buy you a ring and you can wear it in private. But you will know that you're mine."

"I won't forget," she said.

She was branded with it. All the way down to the bone.

"Let's go back."

She almost didn't want to. She wanted to stay here. Naked outside, wild and free.

She felt tender. Like a shield of protection had been stripped away from her, revealing her vulnerabilities, not to him as much as to herself.

But it was confronting.

And she felt quite strongly that she had been through enough recently. She'd had enough character development.

Or maybe she hadn't.

The world had changed around her, but perhaps she had changed herself sufficiently.

"All right," she said. "Let's go back."

They went back to the house and showered. He ended up taking her again when they landed in a heap of tangled limbs in his bed.

She clung to him all night.

She didn't sleep.

When the sun rose the next morning she was still in Dionysus's arms. And she knew that it was the first day for everything would be different.

CHAPTER ELEVEN

HE HAD WON. It was really that simple, and that complicated. His brother was dead, and he had claimed the woman that he had always wanted.

A victory. And not a Pyrrhic one. A complicated one, yes. One that mixed grief and regret with no small amount of triumph. But it was the single greatest achievement of his thirty years.

Ariadne was his.

He woke up each morning holding her in his arms, and he relished it.

When she would walk out of their shared room entirely nude to eat breakfast in the courtyard with the sun shining down on her skin, he gave thanks.

Like a wood nymph. An incredibly sexy one.

He had her.

And you don't know what to do with her.

He shut off that voice inside of himself. He absolutely knew what to do with her. He kept her panting and crying out his name as often as possible. If they had lives at jobs outside of this place, they had both done a good job of forgetting. Yes, they devoted a bit of time to making sure that things weren't on fire. But mostly, they were dedicating themselves to conceiving a baby.

At least, that was how they framed it. In truth, he felt as if they were making up for the lost years. Her, for her virginity which had overstayed its welcome, and him for all the years he had everyone but her.

In this place, it was easy though, to forget that any years had passed at all. It was like that kiss on the balcony had led to this moment, instead of the ten years after, which had been...

He had been dead, basically.

It was why it had been so easy to put everything into starting his company. To put everything into defying his father, and perhaps trying to prove that he was a better man than his brother.

That thought hit him especially hard as he sat there, drinking his coffee and looking at Ariadne's beautiful profile as she sat with her face upturned toward the sun and her eyes closed.

Yes. Maybe a not insignificant part of himself had wanted to prove that the way he had done things was better.

She said Theseus had hated himself.

But Dionysus couldn't say he was an avid fan of his own behavior.

Everything he did came from a place of rage. Anger. Everything he did was about... Her.

Her eyes fluttered open, and she looked at him. "What?"

"I didn't say anything," he said.

"You were thinking. Loudly."

"You can hear my thoughts now?"

"I've always been able to hear your thoughts."

He shook his head. "No. If that were true, then you would have run away from me back then."

"I did run away from you," she said, her words soft. They hit him in a particularly vulnerable place. And the truth they carried had implications that echoed in parts of him he didn't want to examine.

"And now you have nowhere to run to."

"I chose this," she said.

She stood from her chair and came to him, sitting on his lap. He was instantly hard, the feel of her soft, lush body pressed against his more than he could bear.

"Then you are a fool," he said.

"Don't be like that. You want me."

The certainty in her eyes hit him low in the chest.

"You know I do."

He was tangled up in this. In her. What a strange thing to finally have what he craved.

To have what he had wanted all this time.

And still feel like there was something... Missing. Something that he couldn't quite grasp.

"In some respects these past weeks have been the saddest of my life. How could they not be." She looked down, and then, back up at him. "And in other ways, they have been the best. And I don't know how to un-tangle those things from one another."

His heart did something shattering. Something he didn't want to name.

"Why?" He couldn't stop himself from asking. Even if it was selfish. Even if it was a betrayal.

"I have spent my life taking care of myself. Taking care of other people. I loved Theseus. But I see now that I loved him like a sister. I protected him. I was his shield. And I didn't do it because I'm so good, because I'm so altruistic. Far from it. I did it because by building a safe place for him, I built one for myself too. I did it because it made me indispensable in a way that no other relationship could have. By protecting him, I thought I was protecting myself. By protecting him, I thought that I was making sure that I would never end up alone." He watched as tears welled up in her eyes. He found himself angry again at his brother for putting them there. "But since I collapsed at the Diamond Club, you have taken care of me. No one has ever taken care of me before."

He moved toward her. And put his hand on her cheek, just in time to catch a tear that spilled from her eye and tracked downward. "I'm very sorry that I'm your only option for care, Ariadne. You deserve better than that."

Because when had his care ever accomplished much? Historically, it hadn't.

It hadn't been enough to protect Theseus from their father. Hadn't been enough to protect him from the feeling that something was wrong with him. It hadn't been enough to make him want to trust Dionysus with the truth.

"I don't want anyone else."

He would have argued with her, but he didn't have the strength. Because he had wanted her all this time, all these years, and he had never been able to have her. And he did now. It felt selfish, and yet, he couldn't fathom releasing hold on her now.

This was complicated. But he'd lived simply for a very long time. Had pleased no one and nothing but himself.

Part of him had always craved this. The chance to care for her.

He had told her that he had wanted her without end all of this time, and it was true.

But the desire to care for her was even more pronounced. Even more driving than the lust, and that was saying something, because it was quite simply the most powerful need he had ever experienced.

But there was no point discussing that. Because he didn't know how to define these feelings, and the only thing he knew for sure was that if she married him, he would have her. If they had a child together, she would stay.

She had stayed with Theseus all that time out of loyalty to him. She would stay for the loyalty to their child. Of that he was certain.

And in this way, she would hold onto him.

He would have her.

And if he felt a strange sense of disquiet over the truth that Ariadne had been kept for far too long by a man who couldn't give her everything she deserved, he pushed that to the side. She had made her choice. She wanted certain things that pushed him toward demanding this.

She knew what she was getting into.

She was wild like he was. And she had made her choices. She might deserve more than him, but she herself had said she didn't especially want it.

Of course, she had also thought that she didn't need passion.

But there, he was giving her that at least.

He could give her freedom.

That determination bloomed inside of him. "You know that with me you don't need to present the façade of the perfect wife. With me, you get to be the girl you were here."

A smile curved her lips. "Why do you think I'm out here in the sun and nothing else?"

"You are not beholden to those old rules anymore."

She sighed. "I always will be until your father dies. He can always revoke my position at the company."

"And it means that much to you?"

For the first time, a small crease appeared between her brows, and she looked just slightly like she might not know the answer for certain. When before she had been so... Ruthlessly direct. He could see now, though, that she had spent these past years as Theseus's personal Joan of Arc. And with his actions, he had fundamentally tied her to a stake, and put her at risk for being burned alive.

Because she was right. Their father would hold her hostage, endlessly. And to release hold of it would be to let go of all her work. It would be to lay her sword down after all these years in battle.

He could see why she couldn't do that easily. But he wanted her to. But that was where he had to acknowledge the limitation of what he offered her.

If he could be everything, then he would demand everything in return.

But he couldn't.

He didn't deserve to ask for everything.

"As long as I have a place where I can be myself, then I'll be all right. I haven't had that."

That realization broke him. "You said my brother was your best friend. But you... You couldn't be yourself with him?"

"I couldn't be everything with him, no. Because of course we didn't share this. This part of myself was pushed down so far, and it wasn't him. Not only him. He can't shoulder the blame for the decisions that I made. For my fears. I let myself get bogged down in what I saw as my own flaws."

"You thought your passion was a flaw?"

"Yes. So I buried it."

He saw again the image of her in full armor, with a sword.

And he saw her clearly.

"You never repressed your passion, you just channeled it into a different place. You were a warrior for him, all this time. You kept everybody away from the thing he was most ashamed of. You stood between him and all of the enemies that he saw around him."

"Some protector," she said. "He's still gone."

He gripped her chin. "You were the fiercest of protectors. That it ended in a way no one would have wished doesn't change that. Your passion shines too brightly to have ever been suppressed entirely. And passion is more than one thing. Your passion was never dangerous." He leaned toward her, his mouth a whisper from hers. "I envy that. I wanted your passion for myself. Of course, I wanted to use it differently, even if I didn't realize. But you could never have suppressed that. It was what I saw from the beginning. Whether you express it by running freely here, or putting on a suit and going to work, and advocating for the people that you employ, you are all passion, Ariadne Katrakis. And it has served you well. It's what makes you strong." He kissed her then, lightly. "Never forget that."

Ariadne thought about what Dionysus had said to her all day. She thought about her own core beliefs, the way that she thought she had successfully taken her passion and extinguished it. He was right. She had simply channeled it into something else. Relentlessly.

It was why protecting Theseus had become her everything. Because it had become her sole mission. Because she had taken that part of herself that had a constellation of dreams and built the dam, so that it was all contained into one pool. She had done it to protect him. She had done it to protect herself.

And she recognized that it wasn't serving her.

Yes, she wanted to continue her work. But she was going to have to allow her passion to be multifaceted again.

Because she was going to have a husband who...

She looked out at the ocean, feeling the sand between her toes as she walked. It was warm. Perfect. She paused, and relished the feeling of the breeze moving over her skin. The way that it made her dress flutter around her ankles.

She and Dionysus had both declined to label what they were.

But he needed more than protection. So did she. That was one way to keep somebody with you.

But it wasn't them.

When they talked, they were always trying to get beneath the surface of each other's skin. When they touched, it was like they were trying to find a way to melt into one.

He had said he imagined her in armor. That was accurate. Because she had found a way to make sure that nothing much hit her. She couldn't feel it. It bounced right off. That was how she lived in a house with a man who she...

She had cared for him more than he cared for her. It might not have been romantic love, but the realization that the investment had been largely hers was a painful one. So of course, she had learned to walk through the world protected. To make sure that she was keeping herself safe. But she couldn't do that with Dionysus.

That wasn't the relationship they were having. It wasn't one where they lived separate lives with walls both inside and out between them. It wasn't the role of protector and protected.

She couldn't have armor, because she needed to be able to be changed by what they were. By what they were finding with each other. And she found she wanted that. She wanted caring for him, being with him, to change her.

Because of course, she wanted to have a child with him. And if she wanted to have a child, she had to be willing to shift and change for that child as well.

It was hard. To try and shift things that had kept her protected for so long. That had protected her from crumbling.

She had wrapped herself in purpose. And that purpose was protecting Theseus. It had kept her from having to deal with anything too multifaceted, anything too difficult.

It had kept her from having to reckon with that shift and feelings she had experienced with Dionysus.

Dionysus had been her friend. Purely. When they had been younger, that had been all it was.

But as they had gotten older, it had changed. And if Theseus hadn't been there to stand between them, the reckoning would have been...

Well, she was afraid of that reckoning. At least, she had been. Until she had lost her safety, until she had lost her comfort, until it had felt in the moment like she'd had nothing left to lose.

And in that bravery, she had found something brilliant. Something beautiful.

She could feel that there were other steps to take. Steps beyond the ones she had already accomplished.

There was further to go.

But it was just... Even if she could fix her own issues, she couldn't fix his.

No. You can't fix his. He has to do that himself.

Well. That left her with very little in the way of reassurance.

Except that she had been trying to fix other people's problems for a very long time. Or at the very least, act as a Band-Aid for them.

She was struggling. With the realization that there was no safe love.

But without love...what was it?

So if she let go of that. She hadn't been able to protect Theseus from that accident. How could she have?

She couldn't heal Dionysus either.

And if she tried, she would only be back in the exact same situation.

She took a long, solid breath and stopped walking.

She thought about who she had been. Before she had been taught to be different. Before she had been shown how disposable women were to her father. Before she had been taught that she was easy to abandon, by her mother. With Theseus she'd flung herself into earning her place. She'd loved him, he'd loved her. Their friendship had been deep and real and yet she'd had a role to play within that and in many ways she'd found it comforting. It had been a way to make herself useful.

Dionysus had simply existed with her.

They had run together. Swam together. Smiled together. Laughed together.

Somewhere, in that time with him, he had shown her that she was just fine as she was. And yet it was a lesson that she hadn't wanted to learn. A lesson she had been afraid to learn that, for some strange reason or another.

It scared her even now.

She couldn't say why.

She was still enough for him.

Even in the state he was in. He wanted to marry her. He wanted to be with her. And even if that didn't mean love to him, it meant something. Because he didn't have to do that.

What was love, then?

She wished that she had an answer to that. For her, it had meant a lot more giving than receiving.

She thought about what she knew about Dionysus. He loved being outdoors. He was sentimental. He had that car that he had gotten at seventeen. He had this island that had belonged to them. He had that cave, a sanctuary that was quite literally at the heart of the island, and he had built his house around it.

And yet he was alone. So often in his life, he was alone. She wondered if that was why he took so much care with his surroundings. Maybe it was his way of not feeling so alone.

She had been alone too. She understood. The ways that you went about trying to build community. She had done it through the business. She had tried to make her friendship with Theseus enough.

For him it was sex. And solitude.

Two things that didn't go together, not when you were actually trying to foster intimacy. But he wasn't. Because he was afraid of it. With her, he touched the surface of it. As she did with him.

They were like two wary creatures, cautiously circling each other. Wanting to get closer. Not knowing how.

She had an idea. She knew how to cook, she enjoyed it, in fact. It had been a way that she connected with Theseus, when things were good. They would cook a meal together, and share stories about their day.

She gave the household staff the rest of the day off, and drew on her memory of him. Of what they used to eat together when they were young. She found fresh strawberries, and champagne. And she smiled, thinking of that memory of when they had been so reckless together.

She made fish—his favorite, locally caught from around the island—and risotto, which was more to please her. She set out a fruit platter, similar to the one he had made for her when she had first arrived.

She could remember that night well.

And she knew that he was a nostalgic man. So she just had a feeling. She had a feeling that if she looked in her closet, there would be a white dress, similar to the one she had worn on her eighteenth birthday.

She looked through all the dresses, and found the one. Whether he intended it or not—but knowing him he had, it was strikingly like the one she had on that night.

She wanted to find the words. Inside of herself, between them, to express what she wanted. To express what he meant to her. Right now, this wordless seduction would have to do. This digging in to what mattered to him.

And as she put that white dress on, she mentally imagined taking her armor off. She had been working on that. On being unguarded. On being herself, with nothing between them. But tonight, she was doing it deliberately. Tonight, she was reaching for vulnerability, not just accepting it. Because her armor did a good job at keeping wounds at bay. But it also did a good job of keeping everything else out too. And she didn't want that. Not now.

She left her hair loose, just as she had that night.

She and Theseus had announced their engagement that night.

It was a memory she didn't allow herself to have often. She stood there, in front of the mirror, and let it play out.

CHAPTER TWELVE

Ten years ago...

THE ROOM WAS decorated beautifully. It was the most amazing birthday party she had ever had. And the only reason it was happening was because of Theseus. Because Patrocles so approved of their future union, that he had given his home and resources over to the celebration.

It was beautiful, but it could've been for anyone. It wasn't for her specifically. But for any girl her age. That was fine with her.

She didn't know why she felt like grieving.

She didn't know why she felt like her life was ending.

She was resolved in her friendship with Theseus. She loved him. More than anything.

But as she stood there, watching the room filled with people, it wasn't Theseus's face she saw. She knew that most people would think that was insane. Because they were identical.

But they weren't. They simply weren't.

She didn't see Dionysus. Not when the party started.

And not when Theseus took her hand and led her to the front of the room, holding her left hand up, the diamond sparkling there. Not when he announced their engagement.

It would be a long engagement. They wouldn't marry until she was twenty.

She felt like she was spiraling out of control. Because what difference did it make? They could get married tomorrow. It wouldn't change anything. They weren't ever going to kiss, not really. They were never going to make love.

When he did kiss her, there in front of the room, it was dry. And she had to fight to keep from pushing him away, which made her feel instantly guilty. She had agreed to this. Happily. She hadn't been coerced. Not in any fashion.

Afterward, she went out to the balcony.

She walked over to the railing, and put her hands on it. She looked out into the darkness, squinted to see if she could find the sea. Or maybe she was looking to see if she could find Dionysus. She wondered if he was angry.

She hadn't told him about Theseus. He didn't know anything. He would be the one person most likely not to believe it at all. Unless he could really believe that she had kept such an elaborate secret from him. A secret liaison with his brother.

This was the best thing to do. Friendship meant something. It lasted.

It was the only way.

"Ariadne."

She turned sharply, and saw him striding toward her. The look in his eyes was fierce. On fire. He was wearing a white shirt and black pants, just the same as Theseus, but it was so patently not Theseus. And when he moved to her, and caught her up in his arms, there could never have been any doubt.

His mouth was a wildfire. Setting every part of her on fire. His hands moved over her body. And she wanted to weep. She wanted to run, and she wanted to cling to him for as long as she could. To claim this one taste of passion.

"What the hell is going on?"

She heard Theseus. And she pulled away. Sharply.

And then she separated herself from Dionysus, and went to Theseus.

She let herself come back to the present.

She had run away then. Because it had been too much.

It had been too strong.

It had been everything that she wanted. But she had been just… She wanted to be angry at that girl, but mostly she just felt sorry for her.

What a terrible, awful situation to be in. Because what she wanted more than anything was for somebody to be true to her. To honor the promises they had made to her. So she wouldn't have been able to respect herself if she would have broken her word to Theseus. But also, it left her… So much more alone than she had realized. She just hadn't known men. She just hadn't known.

Her heart beat painfully as she walked downstairs, and set the scene on the terrace. It was a different terrace. Just like it was a different night.

It was different, and yet so much the same.

She texted Dionysus to let him know dinner was ready, and then she went to stand with her back to the door, her hands on the railing, her focus out toward the sea.

She heard footsteps behind her.

"Ariadne."

She turned, and it was like those moments melted together. The man he had been, filled with anger and passion and need, right there with the man he was now.

And there was nothing between them.

He took her in his arms and he kissed her. And she kissed him back. With all of the passion and need that she had tried to suppress then.

"Dionysus," she whispered against his mouth, because she would let there be no doubt that she knew exactly who he was.

Exactly what she was doing.

She knew. Of course she did.

The kiss was a burning wildfire, and it was like she had a second chance. To burn because she chose to. To burn because she wanted this, and wanted him more than anything.

The reason that she was here was lost.

All the sadness, all the grief, all the years apart lost in that moment.

She clung to him, and kissed him from the depths of her very soul.

Because she wouldn't run away. Not this time. She had a chance to do it differently. She had a chance to make a different choice.

"Dinner is lovely," he growled against her mouth. "But I have to have you."

"Yes."

Because this was how that night should have ended. She should have chosen him then. She should have.

As he picked her up, sweeping her off her feet and carrying her in the house, up the stairs, she felt like she was living in those two moments. And what might've been and what was.

At least he was here now.

He was here holding her now.

He felt it too, she knew that he did. Knew that this was more than just another coming together. It was a reclamation. A reckoning.

It was their chance to start again. To explore what might've been.

It is. It isn't just what might've been. You get to make a different choice.

You get to choose him.

Her heart felt like it had wings, lifting her chest. He stripped her dress from her body, and cast it to the floor. And she took her time baring his body to her own hungry gaze.

He was everything.

She said his name like an incantation, over and over again. It had always been him.

The moment that she had met him, it had been like all the pieces of her life had fallen into place. Theseus had been by his side, and Theseus had been vulnerable. He appealed to her, because he needed her. She had turned away from her clear and obvious fate because she had been too afraid. And when he had been the braver of the two of them, when he had pulled her into his arms, she had walked away. She had run away. Because she had been too frightened to do anything else.

Because Dionysus could truly hurt her.

With Theseus, she had chosen a clear path that she could see the end of.

And he had never had the power to shatter her.

It was devastating to admit that. Even to herself. She had cared for him, but what she had chosen was safety. Not in the way that she had imagined. It wasn't just about a sense of physical security, or even companionship. It was that there were two paths in front of her. And one had the potential to be wild and glorious. But she had chosen safety, not over potential heartbreak, but over potential joy. Because she hadn't felt like she was worthy.

Had she always felt like she wasn't enough?

And then she had been grappling with it all over

again while life had taken Theseus from her. Had taken
the first pregnancy from her. But she was still here.
And so was Dionysus. And just like that, she felt like
she was enough. She felt like she deserved everything.

Truly.

She took a great gasp of air, trying to do something
about the sharp pain in her chest. Because this hurt as
much as it healed.

But then Dionysus kissed her again, his firm mouth
grounding her to the spot, making her feel breathless.
Weightless. And wholly secure all at the same time.

She ran her hands over his muscular body. Committed every inch of him to memory.

He was hers. He was hers and she wanted him so
very badly.

What was love?

He wanted her just like she was.

He was the only one. Who seemed to want every
part of her. Who seemed to think that she was enough,
just as she was.

He loved her.

She knew it. As sure and certain as she knew where
the sea was just beyond the courtyard. As sure as she
knew the path to the oasis that they loved to swim in.
He loved her.

And she loved him too.

It was why she had run away from him. Because
that terrified her. The real truth was she was afraid of
being in love alone. So she had chosen a man that she

could never truly fall in love with, who could never fall in love with her, so that she could never be blindsided by what she was lacking. She had chosen half, because she didn't want to try to carry the whole of it and fail.

She had chosen it.

She was done. She wanted all. She wanted every-thing. She wanted him.

And everything that meant.

She kissed her way down his body, found herself on her knees before him, and encircled his hard, mascu-line length in her hand. She moved her head forward, and took the head of him between her lips, tasting him, but more than that, telling him how she felt. How much she loved him. How much she wanted him.

"Only you," she whispered as she slid her tongue along his shaft.

She pleasured him like that until he gripped her hair. Until he hauled her to her feet and kissed her. Driv-ing her back against the wall, where he thrust into her hard, holding her thigh up over his hip as he took her over and over again.

As he reminded her that they were the only ones that were like this.

This was passion.

And for the two of them, this was the only passion there can ever be.

She felt replete with it. Bursting with it.

It was absolutely everything.

And she gave herself up to the joy of it, clinging to

his shoulders and crying out his name as she found her release. As he roared out his own, clinging to her, pulsing deep within her.

"I love you," she whispered.

But then he let go of her. And he took a step back.

The look in his eyes was wild. Confused. And she knew that she had done something wrong. She knew that… She had made a misstep.

No. You didn't.

She had to say it. She'd had to tell the truth, even if he couldn't handle it. Even if it would end badly.

She had to, because she was done living with half. Done living in the darkness.

"Dionysus, I love you."

He turned away from her, the muscles on his broad back shifting as he put his face in his hands for a moment.

"Did I say something wrong? Because I thought that between us there was no wrong thing to say."

"Ariadne." He turned to face her, his eyes wild, haunted. "You don't have to say that. You don't have to do this, just because you agreed to marry me."

"Why do you think the marriage has anything to do with this?"

"I don't think that you want to get married again for any reason other than love. And… You're right. I shouldn't have made demands of you. Not when I wasn't ready to give you everything. I can't do that to you again."

"You love me," she said, the words coming from a deep, convicted place inside of her.

"It isn't enough."

"Of course it's enough. You are enough for me."

"That isn't what I mean," he said, his face suddenly going cold and remote. "I couldn't give you what you wanted back then, if I could have you wouldn't have married him. Not even to protect him."

"I didn't choose him over you," she said, pain lancing her chest. "Not like that. You know that. I chose fear over you. That is true. But I'm done with that now. I'm not choosing fear anymore."

"It's already done. And it can't ever be that way between us. And the fact that you think it can is why this has to be over. You chose him. And that's all there is to it."

"I am choosing you now," she said. "I'm choosing you because this was what I was too afraid to take then."

"If my brother hadn't died we never would've had this."

"I don't think that's true."

Her chest felt like it had been caved in. "I don't think it's true. Because I really do believe that we would've found a way to each other eventually. You're my fate, Dionysus. I really believe that. I have been… Untangling this for weeks now. Maybe even for years. Spinning it all out inside of me. There's a reason that you were the person that I went to that day at the club."

"You were joining the club. It wasn't as if it was magic that you were there."

"You were my touchstone. You were the only way forward that I could see. You were the only person that I wanted to be with. Don't you understand that? You terrified me then. Not just passion, but you. Because if I couldn't have you, then I was afraid that life wouldn't be worth living for me. And I was happier to take half and feel safe."

"And what changed?"

He was challenging her. Like she didn't actually know what had changed. She did.

"I did. I changed. I realized what I was doing to myself. I realized that I was letting all of the bad things in my life decide how good my life was going to be, and I don't want that anymore. I realized that I was happier loving the people around me more than they loved me, and I don't want that anymore." She looked at him directly. "So if you can't love me as much as I love you, then I will walk away, because I'm not going to live like that anymore."

"Why are you risking everything now?"

Because everything was different. They were different. And the same. Far too much the same and it had to change. It needed to. She had been too afraid of risk ten years ago. She had been afraid of being hurt.

But she'd lost her best friend. He had died right before he'd gotten to step into his truth.

What tribute would it be if she didn't learn from him? What good would it do?

She had to live in her truth. Just as Dionysus needed to learn to live in his.

They had the kind of love that could easily live in the light, why be afraid? Why hide?

For Theseus, for all the love she still felt for him, she couldn't hide.

She should have been honest with him. She should have been honest with herself.

She'd never go back to lying. Not now.

"Because. Because I matter. I do. And you have only yourself to blame for that realization. Because you treated me like I was a whole person from the moment that we met. You were waiting for me to do something interesting. You didn't need me to do you a favor. You didn't need me to rescue you. You loved me the way that I was. Even if it was just as a friend, Dionysus, though I don't think that's the case. Realizing that, looking back at everything with clear focus, that showed me what I want. I want to find my way back to that. I want... I want for us to be together. Really. But I can't heal you. You have to heal you. The reason that I didn't feel like I was enough for Theseus was that I thought it was my job to love him in a way he couldn't love himself. I thought that I was holding him together, but you simply cannot do that for another person. I can't. You can't."

She took a deep, shuddering breath. "I have to let you find your own way in this. And I'm brave enough to do it. Because I would rather risk everything to get what we're both worth, than go along with half. Ever again. That night… That night when you kissed me on my birthday, I ran away from you. I wish that I hadn't. I wanted to give you a night where I didn't run. So I want to make it very clear that I am not running away from you. I'm giving you space. So that you can decide what you're going to do next. So that you can decide if you want to heal, because one thing I know for sure, I cannot sit there in hope that I will be enough to heal someone ever again. I need you to do it. I need you to find that in yourself."

She felt shattered. She felt… Devastated. But she had to do this.

"I love you, Dionysus. And that's why I have to leave you. Even if you don't understand that, it's the truth." She blinked back tears. "I'm going to go pack. And then I'm going to call my pilot and have him come and get me."

"Oh, yes. Of course you have a pilot now as well."

"I'm one of the richest people in the world," she said. She blinked hard. "But right now I feel like I don't have anything. It's terrifying. But I would rather be terrified and know that I was demanding nothing less than what I deserve."

She turned and she left him. It was the hardest thing that she had ever done.

Her chest felt like it was caving in, as she made the phone call. As she waited.

Finally, she walked down to the beach, with her one bag of belongings, and boarded the plane.

She was leaving the island. She was leaving Dionysus.

She was leaving behind her hopes and dreams.

This was bravery. And it was terrible.

But she knew that it was the only way that things could ever be all right in the end. The only way they could ever be more than all right.

She knew what happened when you sit in an old wound and let it fester. She knew what happened when you didn't do the hard work of healing.

And she loved Dionysus too much to consign him to that fate.

She loved herself too much.

She cried all the way back to England.

Life had been especially unkind to her recently.

And this had been her choice.

She could only hope that in the end everything worked out as best it could.

She could only hope, that in the end, she had his love.

Because if not, she knew that nothing would ever be the way that it was supposed to be.

Dionysus was her fate.

But he was going to have to do the work so that they could both claim it.

CHAPTER THIRTEEN

HE SAT IN the grotto at the back of his house. He looked at the soft glow of the salt lamp in the corner. And then he stood up and turned it on its side. The salt shattered into millions of pieces.

He did the same with the other and watched it go to pieces. A spray of rose-colored failure all around the floor.

Where was the healing? He hadn't seen it yet. He hadn't even come close.

Nothing in him was healed. Everything was broken. Fractured and ruined.

She loved him. She claimed that she loved him.

But no one had ever… No one had ever stayed with him. No professions of love had ever been enough. Why would this one?

She had chosen his brother over him. But that wasn't what he was truly afraid of. He had been a bastard, and he knew that.

He had been unnecessarily cruel to her. But he had done it to protect himself.

Because…

Because he had taken his father's fists for Theseus. He had stood in between the two of them. He had been a target so that Theseus could remain unscathed. And it hadn't been enough.

Theseus had stolen Ariadne from him.

He hadn't even loved her. Not like Dionysus had. But there was something about him that made what he wanted unimportant. He had thought that he and Ariadne had connected, but she had chosen Theseus.

Nothing that he did, no part of him, had ever been sufficient. She said that he loved her as she was, but when had she done the same for him?

She said that she was afraid.

Yes, she had. She had said that. But she had… She had utterly destroyed him. When what he had endured losing her had been unthinkable. He…

And you're losing her again. To what end?

If he didn't lose her now, he would eventually. He would lose her over and over again. Because that was how it was with everyone.

He had never seen love in his life that had lasted. He had never seen love in a way that endured. There was not a single connection, not blood or water that seemed to stand up in his life.

What was he supposed to think. He had no example of love lasting. He had no example of him being worthy.

Ariadne had just taken a risk. She had laid everything down for him.

And still…

Still.

He had his island. He had his cave.

That would be enough.

All of this has been a replacement of her. And you know it.

All of it. He had built this house, he had built this cave, where he used to go to hide from his father's violent moods.

He had structured this entire place around finding some sanity without her. Finding something that held him to the earth.

And now he was left with only this place, and it felt utterly insufficient. It was nothing, and so was he.

Without her.

She took a risk. Why can't you?

It wasn't enough.

No. So far, it hadn't been enough. But neither had this place. Neither had his salt lamps. He laughed, bitterly. Because everything had been a bandage, on a mortal wound. Everything had been a pointless, useless exercise, trying to piece together a life that felt like something without Ariadne in it, and now he could have her, and he wasn't claiming her.

Now he was being a coward.

She had said that she wanted to re-create that kiss. Re-create the moment where she had chosen to walk away, and stay instead.

But the truth of it was, he hadn't gone after her then. He had never said everything that was in his heart.

He had been a coward.

At the first sign that she might not feel the same, he had fallen back.

Rather than ripping himself open.

She had done it over again. He had to do the same.

He stood there, frozen, in the middle of his ruined grotto.

Because the grotto had only ever been a mirror of his soul. Hollow and lonely. And now broken.

He would have her.

He would.

He would go after her, and he would tell her how he felt. Because of course he loved her.

Thinking that fixed something inside of him. Something he hadn't fully realized was broken. Oh, he knew that much was broken inside of him. But he hadn't realized that what he truly needed was her love. And to love her in return.

But she was right. He already did.

Railing against it was futile.

He loved her.

And if he didn't claim her, then he would be the author of his own misery. He would finally have to blame himself, like he should have done years ago.

Because she might have walked away, but he had let her go.

And he wouldn't make that mistake again.

He loved Ariadne.

And she would be his wife.

She would be his love.

Because she was everything. And he was finally willing to admit it.

When her period failed to come, she wasn't shocked, so much as resigned.

She was pregnant. With Dionysus's baby. And she could carry on the way that she had intended to. She could carry on the way that they had started.

But she wasn't going to do that.

She had lost Dionysus, so nothing else really mattered. She was going to have to be billed.

All she had was herself, and she was... She was embracing it. The terror of it. The beauty.

She had no other choice. This was what living bravely felt like. This was what being true to herself felt like. It was hard.

But this was what she needed to do. This was the only way she was ever going to become the kind of mother that her child deserved. The best mother that she could be.

She wasn't afraid. She wasn't afraid anymore that she wouldn't know how.

Because she knew that she could grow. And change. She knew she could be braver and better.

She was proud, and she was happy in some ways for the girl that she had been.

Even if she was wretchedly sad for the woman she was now in other ways.

But she had a meeting scheduled with Patrocles. And she was ready.

He still kept an office in the main building of Katrakis Shipping. And she was ushered in immediately. Where he sat behind the desk. He was small now. Shrunken with age. And it amazed her just how much trouble this one, small, shriveled man had caused. Once, he had been feared. And now... He had lost his oldest son. A son he had never truly known, because he was such a horrible man. And she could throw that back in his face now. But he would never understand. He would never see it. Because he would never grow. That he would never change.

He would never do the work he needed to do to become a decent human being.

"Ariadne. You have been off the radar for some time."

"I've been dealing with some things. I have to tell you. I had a miscarriage."

He looked up at her, his eyes sharp. "That is a shame."

"Yes. But I am pregnant again."

"Good. I had thought that Theseus might have left behind insurance."

She shook her head. "No. It isn't Theseus's child. It's Dionysus's."

Because she would never deny who the father of this baby was, no matter what happened between them. She was going to tell him next. It didn't matter that they couldn't be together, she would give him a chance to be a father. She knew that he would be a wonderful father.

"Dionysus," said Patrocles. "That changes things."

"I thought it might. And it's all right if it does. If you take everything from me, I don't care. I'm not playing your games anymore. Theseus and I lived our lives trying to please you. It was so important to him. I'm not going to do that anymore. I don't care about you. I care about this company. And I care about the people in it. I think you should let me continue to run it because I do a great job. I could've lied to you. And I could've told you that this was Theseus's baby. You would never have known. Science wouldn't have been able to prove otherwise. But that would just be giving you more power than you deserve. You don't deserve any."

"Then you will not keep this company."

"I thought you might say that. But know this, I have a plan to expand things over the next few years, and if you keep things going the way that you were running them before Theseus took over, the company is going to die. You are welcome to cut me off as a sop to your pride. You lose your legacy. You'll lose everything. So it's up to you. Be spiteful, and cold, as we all know you are. Cut off your own legacy to spite your face. Or let me have it. Let me continue on in the work Theseus was going to do. The work that I planned to do. After all, we will still be connected by a child. Whether either of us want that to be true or not."

She turned and walked out of the office, but stopped. "I hope you know, that your sons are two of the finest men ever to be born into the world. I love Theseus. But all he really cared about was being good enough, and he never thought he was. He was. He was good enough just like he was. And so is Dionysus. He has always been my friend. He has always been… You don't give him any credit. But he built a life for himself completely apart from you. And that must be why you dislike him so much. He set out to prove that he didn't need you. And he did it. Spectacularly. As much as I love Theseus, in the end, it's Dionysus that I want to be. Because he proves just how useless you are."

And then she did walk out, her breath leaving her body in a painful gust.

She had done it. She had potentially cut everything off. And it was a gamble. One that terrified her. Because maybe it wouldn't pay off. Maybe she had just condemned all the workers in that company.

She would start again. She would hire all of them. That was exactly what she would do. She didn't need to lean on anybody.

She would make her own legacy.

Her own Katrakis legacy.

In honor of everything Theseus could have been.

In honor of everything Dionysus was.

Because her child would know about both of them.

When her child learned about the heritage of being a Katrakis, she would make sure that it meant something good.

And she would be a part of that.

She swept out of the building, and walked back toward her townhouse.

She didn't know how she was going to hold herself together. She was shaking. She wanted to call Dionysus. Well. She had to. She had to tell him about the baby.

She walked into the lobby of her building. And she saw him. His back turned away from her.

It was just like that night, on the balcony.

When she was eighteen.

Except their positions were reversed.

And she found herself striding toward him, all of her need, all of her passion, rising up inside of her. "Dionysus."

He turned, and she grabbed him, kissing him, for all the world to see. And she knew that they still had so many things left to be said between them.

She knew that she shouldn't be doing this, that she had taken a firm stance on love, or nothing. But she needed to touch him. This was honest.

And she had vowed not to turn away from these kinds of moments.

So she didn't.

"Ariadne," he said, his voice hoarse.

"You're here."

"Of course I am. I had to come for you. I had to. Ariadne, I love you."

Her heart hit her breastbone hard. "You love me?"

"Yes. I was a fool, and I was a coward. I was so... I didn't know what love was, Ariadne. I had no idea what it looks like. I knew that what I felt for you was real, but I didn't know what it could be.

"I was afraid. I was afraid of what it would look like to lose you. But then I did. And… I have never felt like I was enough for anyone."

"Please," she said, holding his hands. "I need you to understand. It wasn't that you weren't enough. You were too much. You were so much that I was overwhelmed with it, overflowing with it. So I ran away. But I'm not running anymore. I'm not." She took a deep breath. "I'm pregnant. And I told your father. I told him it was your baby. I think I've lost everything."

He stood there, looking stunned. "You… You're pregnant?"

"Yes."

"You little fool. Why did you tell him that I was the father?"

"Because you are. Because I'm proud that you're the father of my baby. And I'm proud that you're the love of my life. Because I wanted him to know. Because I wanted everyone to know. Because… Because I was committed. To being brave. To being honest. I am not hiding away parts of myself to stay safe anymore. So I am very, very not safe and I'm so glad that you're here."

He gathered her up in his arms. "You're not running. But I came after you. To tell you that I loved you, even then. To tell you that I have done everything in the intervening years to try and convince myself that I didn't need you. But I did. You were always what was missing.

You are my fate, Ariadne. You are right about that. Because nothing was ever quite so perfect as it was when we were together. And we didn't find this as soon as we might have. But we have it now. We have it now."

"I love you."

"And I love you. Always."

It had started in the Diamond Club, with that empty chair. Or perhaps it had truly started here, all those years ago. But one thing she knew for certain was that she loved Dionysus Katrakis with all of her soul.

And there was no room at all for fear.

EPILOGUE

WHEN ARIADNE FOUND out that she was pregnant with triplets, she had some strong words for her husband. Only the Katrakis genes could be blamed for such a thing.

They had married quickly. They didn't care about what the world thought, not anymore.

And there were rumors, of course there were. But she didn't care.

The pregnancy with the triplets was surprisingly uneventful, though she did have to stay in bed for most of it. And it wasn't until Androcles, Adonis and Achilles were eight, that she was back to being a rightful member of the Diamond Club, on her own merit.

Her new shipping empire had absolutely smashed Katrakis. She had hired all the employees from Katrakis and given them raises.

In the end, she had bought the struggling company from Patrocles. The payoff that she gave him was nothing compared to what the company had been worth at one time.

It felt like justice.

As did making James godfather to the triplets, and ensuring he was the beneficiary of most of Theseus's wealth. They also brought him on as CFO of their company.

When he joined the Diamond Club some years on, it created the most delightful ripple in the staid institution.

It was also a particularly bittersweet joy to finally inter Theseus's ashes with a grave marker that truly honored him.

Beloved partner to James
Dearest friend of Ariadne
Most loved brother of Dionysus

James and Dionysus had become very fast friends, and though part of her would always mourn that Dionysus hadn't known Theseus fully, in the way she had, she loved that he got to know him through James.

And when James found love again ten years later they and the triplets were in the wedding.

Identical boys, and all menaces.

She loved them.

As she loved her husband. They were busy, of course, but they always found time for each other. They always took time out on the island.

They brought their children, who ran around and swam and played.

And one night, they snuck down to swim, just the two of them. Like they were young, and like they were themselves. She swam up to her husband, and wrapped her arms around his neck, kissing him. "Do you know," she said. "I'm the richest woman in the world."

"I had heard that," he said.

"It isn't the money," she said. "It's us."

"Ah," he said. "Something we can agree on."

* * * * *

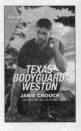